"*Aquamarine* is a warm, daringly original novel about the many possible lives of its complex heroine. Carol Anshaw writes with an unsparing, observant eye, captivating wit, and great compassion. Her novel is one of the most unusual and memorable I've read in a long time."
— Stephen McCauley

"Anshaw's vision is so generous and all-encompassing . . . we're left . . . with the feeling that human beings are so complicated and interesting that we all could have ended up anywhere, doing anything . . . Anshaw seems to have had a lot of fun writing this book, and it's a delight to read." — *Voice Literary Supplement*

"Anshaw creates a very real, very moving world full of wonderful characters and beautifully written moments." — *San Francisco Examiner*

"Carol Anshaw . . . writes with biting humor and a touching reverence for the power of loss. Jesse's three lives, buffeted about by choices both right and wrong, are unveiled with . . . a vivid spirit that highlights Anshaw's craft . . . And in that somber moment after closing this remarkable book, we look back on our own lives, and wonder." — *Boston Globe*

"A novel built on a premise as fresh and provocative as it is beautifully realized . . . [Anshaw] excels in astute, pithy asides that sum up character and situation." — *Publishers Weekly*

"Richly textured . . . The way that Anshaw juggles her characters . . . is magical." — *Rocky Mountain News*

"There are a million wonderful things to say about this book. The best parts are the delicate delineations of friendship and love between women, and the absolutely radiant portrait of woman as athlete, as splendidly competent physical being. I loved *Aquamarine*!" — Carolyn See

"Fresh and unfettered . . . Anshaw . . . is as clever as she is original . . . Anshaw tells each of these three stories with appealing naturalness, touches of wry humor and a gift for characterization."
— *Los Angeles Times*

"Bittersweet . . . inventive and well written." — *Ms.*

"This fantasy novel turns on a powerful philosophical notion . . . Giving Jesse multiple yet consistent identities proves to be a psychological tour de force." — *Glamour*

"An imaginative, original work." — *Kirkus Reviews*

"On first read, *Aquamarine* so captured my imagination that I found myself wishing I could buy a dozen copies and start a discussion group, just so I'd be able to debate all the questions this astonishing novel provokes about the nature of the individual and her power to determine the course of her life." — Dorothy Allison

"A stylish, well-crafted, substantial entertainment." — *Booklist*

"Anshaw's generous character development, her engaging style and her platinum observations on contemporary life make *Aquamarine* a stand-up, standout book." — *Kansas City Star*

"Winning and witty." — *Orlando Sentinel*

"Anshaw has written a wise and daring book. Anyone grappling with the 'what-ifs' of middle or approaching middle age is likely to find it poignant, engaging, provocative." — *Belles Lettres*

"*Aquamarine* is extremely readable and bounces along engagingly, energized by its warmhearted sympathies and its lively wit."
— *New York Newsday*

"*Aquamarine* should delight anyone who has ever wondered 'what if?' . . . What if you had taken a different job, married someone else, had children or not had children . . . Anshaw did more than wonder 'what if?'; she made a delightful book about it." — *Detroit News/Free Press*

"*Aquamarine* is as dazzling as the gemstone, as cool as deep water. Carol Anshaw has both flash and substance." — Rita Mae Brown

"*Aquamarine* is a stylish, slick little candy-coated gem of a book . . . Welcome Carol Anshaw into your head and onto your bookshelf as a serious novelist — from whom we hope we will see a lot more fine work spring." — *Lambda Book Report*

"Anshaw has an eye for the telling image that pinpoints character, or the mood or metaphor, like the 'aquamarine' of a swimming pool, that evokes a place or an emotion. Although her structure is unconventional, her story is down to earth, funny, and warm. It invites us to enter not just one world, but three, which are plausible and entertaining."
— *Washington Post Book World*

"This is a swift, tender, highly intelligent book — an original theme, a strong voice . . . vigorous and humane." — Shirley Hazzard

Aquamarine

CAROL ANSHAW

Aquamarine

A MARINER BOOK
HOUGHTON MIFFLIN COMPANY
Boston New York

For information about permission to reproduce selections from
this book, write to Permissions, Houghton Mifflin Company,
215 Park Avenue South, New York, New York 10003.

Library of Congress Cataloging-in-Publication Data

Anshaw, Carol.
Aquamarine / Carol Anshaw.
p.   cm.
ISBN 0-395-58562-7
ISBN 0-395-87755-5 (pbk.)
I. Title.
PS3551.N7147A94   1992   91-27963
813'.54—dc20   CIP

Printed in the United States of America

Book design by Robert Overholtzer

QUM 10 9 8 7 6 5 4 3 2 1

Note: The actual hundred-meter freestyle event at the
1968 Olympics had its own setting, and was won and lost
by real-life women, who don't enter into this story. All
characters and events in these pages are purely imagined.

The author gratefully acknowledges permission to quote
from the lyrics of the following songs: "Cheek to Cheek."
© Copyright 1935 by Irving Berlin. © Copyright renewed.
International Copyright Secured. All Rights Reserved.
Lyric excerpt reprinted by permission of Irving Berlin
Music Company. "Open All Night," copyright © 1982
by Bruce Springsteen/ASCAP. All rights reserved.
Used by permission.

For Barbara

ACKNOWLEDGMENTS

I'd like to thank my agent Jean Naggar,
my editor Janet Silver,
and the Ragdale Foundation.

Also, my deep appreciation to
Rebecca Chekouras, Lyn DelliQuadri,
Chap Freeman, Chris Paschen,
Johanna Steinmetz, Claire Whitaker
and — always and most
especially — Mary Kay Kammer.

Freestyle

FOR A FEW supersaturated moments, Jesse feels and sees and smells and hears everything. The crushing heat, the Mexican sky white with a flat sun, pressing like an iron against the roll of her shoulders. The rising scent of chlorine and baby oil and something that's not sweat exactly, but an aquatic analog, something swimmers give off in the last few minutes before an event, a jazzy mix of excitement and fear and wanting. The crowd, riled up as though they are going to swim this race themselves.

Except for her godmother, who sits in the stands, unruffled, unflapped — a midwestern Buddha, here by way of two days and a long night on a Trailways bus from Missouri. With her is Jesse's brother, bouncing a little in his seat, twiddling his hands like a haywire backup singer, a Temptation gone kaflooey. There's so much else going on, though, that for once he draws no particular attention.

Down at pool level with Jesse is Bud Freeman, coach of the American women's team, a crew-cut fireplug several

inches shorter than Jesse, at the moment casually pepper-
ing her arm with light jabs of his thick finger, reminding
her that Marty Finch is a splash-out-and-die girl, not to
worry about her in the first fifty meters. His mouth is so
close to Jesse's face she can smell his breath, which is like
oranges. She nods and tongues the insides of her goggles
and looks over his shoulder at Marty, who is doing leg
stretches against the next starting block, not looking at
Jesse. Which is smart. Jesse shouldn't be looking at her
either, not now.

Jesse stands next to the Lane 4 starting block. She's still
nodding at whatever Bud is saying, although she has
stopped listening, doesn't really need to. She has swum this
race in her head every day since she was fourteen. For most
of those three years' worth of days, her body has been
through fifteen thousand meters, so it will know on its own
precisely how to take these hundred. Today she will really
just be going along with herself for the ride.

It's time to take to the blocks. In this instant, the wave
she was riding — absorbing everything at once — crashes
onto the shore of her self, and she whites out into a space
at her dead center. She loses Bud, the crowd, the sun. All
there is is her and the water stretching out in front of her,
to be gotten through. Fifty meters up. Flip. Fifty meters
back. A quick trip.

She stretches the strap of her goggles around the back of
her head, lets it snap. Fiddles with the eye cups, tugs at the
strap ends until she's sure she has a seal. She crouches and
swings her arms behind her, then forward, just short of
losing her balance. She's ready. She doesn't even need to
see the starter to know he's raising the pistol. She can feel
the event approaching, feel herself moving into it.

"Swimmers, take your marks." The metallic command

comes through the public address horns, taking the event out of the dimension of not-happening, onto the plane of about-to-happen.

She hyperventilates to expand her lungs, flattens her soles against the roughed surface of the block. Now comes the critical moment, the one in which she needs to leave even herself behind and become purely what she can do, translate matter into energy, become velocity. In the hundreds of events she has swum on the way to this one, this split second in which she can see the race ahead completely, and see herself winning it, has given her an edge.

This time, though, the power of belief slips away, just a little. Just for the microslice of the second it takes for her to look over at Marty. Who does, for a flash instant, look back. But, through her goggles and then Marty's, and with the sun behind her blacking her out, Jesse can't read her face. She is still trying to decipher it, to pull some important message off it, still trying to link today with last night, to figure out the connection between those events and this one. While she is temporarily lost in this constellation of fear and exhilaration and squeezed hope, the starter's pistol, which she is supposed to respond to instinctively, as though it's inside her, goes off in some very faraway place. Taking her completely by surprise.

And so Jesse Austin leaps out, hangs suspended for a freeze-frame moment, and enters Olympic waters one tenth of a second later than she should. She can't curse the lapse. There's no time. The next minute is an aquamarine blur. The color shattered into a million wavy panes as the water prisms the sunlight that hits the pool bottom. Aquamarine and the deep blue of the wide stripe she follows down the center of the lane, tucking into her flip turn, where the stripe dead-ends in a T. The touch of painted concrete against the balls of her feet as she pushes off. And then the last fifty. She knows she's swimming fast, maybe faster than she ever has. She feels an infinitesimal difference. It's as though the water has given in, is letting her through.

And then, there's the slick slap of tile on the palm of her hand as she finishes where she started. She comes up fast and flushed and eating air. She corkscrews out of the water, ripping off her goggles, looking around wildly for signs. To her left, in Lane 5, Marty has also touched. She's pulling off her cap with a rubbery squeak, bending back, her hair catching the water like white seagrass. Jesse watches this for a moment; it's a part of the too much happening all at once. She's still looking for the word to come down.

Then Bud is crouching on the rim of the pool just above her, shaking his head, holding up two fingers. She has come in second, taken the silver. Won something, but it's the loss that hits her first. She feels as though great weights are dragging her under. She looks over and watches Marty catch the good news from Ian Travers, the Australian coach. She has taken the gold. She's tossing her cap and goggles into the air and smiling with her whole body. And then she looks around and reaches outside the perimeter of her victory, over the lane markers to wrap an arm around Jesse's shoulders. It's a cross-chest carry of sorts, a gesture to bring Jesse up with her.

Amazingly, it works. Jesse can feel her spirit grabbing onto Marty's, and for this moment at least believes *they've* won, that together they've beat out the competition, that the two of them are laughing together in the hilarious ozone just above the plane of regular mortals. They go under, somersault, come up, and shoot out of the water, trailing arcs of spray behind them.

Jesse feels they have attained a great height, as though glory is a wide, flat place they will inhabit forever, rather than a sharp peak that will quickly slide them down another side, to ground level. But she isn't looking down now, only out, toward the limitless possibilities implicit in having attained this one.

She can feel their breezes rushing over her, lightly.

Skywriter

"SWEETHEART." Neal braces himself in the kitchen doorway, rocking in and out a little as he says, "Can you close the cave? I'm almost done tallying up in the office." His T-shirt is sweat-stuck to his rib cage. He pulls off his baseball cap and wipes his forehead with the inside of his arm. This is the hottest summer down here in anyone's memory. It has cleared a hundred every noon for the past six days. Even the really old folks, who can usually top the present with some dramatic weather of the past, say no, this is the worst hot spell ever.

Jesse nods sure, blots a thread of perspiration from her temple, and releases her hair from the clip at the base of her neck. It whooshes out like a fan. She gathers it and reclips it tightly. "I should just get this mop cut off."

Neal looks at her for a moment as if he sees her, but with the sound off. Then he tunes in. "Don't think of it. Red hair's hard to come by. Yours is your crowning glory."

"I hope you never stop flattering me," Jesse says, and

turns to finish dissolving the lump of canned lemonade in a scarred plastic pitcher, spinning it around with a spatula. The baby inside her kicks, connecting with the handle of the spatula, knocking it out of her hand. She and Neal both look down at the gray rubber blade, centered in a puddle on the old linoleum. And then at the surprise in each other's eyes.

"Do you think this says something about her starter personality?" Jesse says. There are moments when it hits her that she and this baby inside her have yet to meet.

"You mean, even if we send her to some fancy school and teach her which fork to use and how to address invitations, is she still going to wind up punching guys' lights out in bars?"

"We can hope," Jesse says. "I love the idea that she might already be a little scrapper in there." She reaches for the roll of paper towels standing on the counter, but Neal gets there first and begins mopping up while she rinses her hands, wipes them down the skirt of her seersucker maternity smock, pushes open the screen door of the house, and steps outside.

The house started off as two mobile homes set together, but with the passing of time and the addition of a back room and a jalousied side porch and a small patch of front yard bordered by Jesse's rosebushes, it almost passes for a real house. The roses hold it down, give it weight with their sweep of brilliant reds, hybrid tea roses tagged with names of celebrity and importance. Kentucky Derby. Dolly Parton. Chrysler Imperial. The house is set back on the property in a small stand of trees, up a roped-off dirt drive away from the cave and its visitors, out of earshot of the stalactite xylophone, which pulses "Lady of Spain" and "Que Será,

Será" up through the soles of those walking the ground above it.

The cave belongs to Neal's family, the Pratts. They are mostly invested in traveling carnivals but have a few stationary attractions like this and Lookout Point at the western edge of the state, plus a small geyser in Arkansas. Billed as Pratt's Caverns, it's an old-fashioned sight. In the spring, two guys came by and tried to talk Neal into putting in a laser show. He wasn't interested. He likes the cave fine just the way it is. He sometimes refers to it as "majestic." One of the things about him which first caught Jesse's notice was this capacity for corniness. He really reads the verses inside birthday cards. He sings along at concerts, and with the car radio.

This is the height of their tourist season, and in this heat, the natural coolness of the cave makes it even more attractive. Today they had more than two hundred people going through, including two tour buses of Germans early in the afternoon. The entrance has been shut for over an hour now. Before they can close up entirely, though, someone has to check to make sure all the caverns are empty. Sometimes local school kids sneak in, try to stay the night to see if the place is haunted. Once in a while, old people wander off from their tours, grow confused, get a little lost.

The steps are so worn at the center, it looks as though the stone is sagging. Jesse follows them down, holding on to the rail — something she never did before the baby. She is used to being physically reckless. Now she has to behave like a courier of valuable goods.

As many times as she has been down here, she always gets a small thrill when she first comes out of the low entrance tunnel into the main cavern, where the stone turns slick and opens wide, like a yawn. She feels she is standing inside the mouth of a giant petrified creature from an earlier chapter of time. She likes to hear the sighs of surprise pass through the huddled clusters of tourists as they come upon this underground cathedral. Anyone seeing it for the first time feels like the first person seeing it, ever. It brings out the explorer in people. For those so inclined, there's a religious cast to the experience.

She shuts down lights as she goes, rattles bar handles on the exit doors, drags her fingertips along the cool, moist, smooth walls. On her way out, she passes the Azure Grotto, washed in blue floods. She'd like to go in and sit for a while, make the blue go to aquamarine. Drop in on the past. But it's dinnertime now, and she has to see to the people in her present. She goes to fetch her brother.

William helps out in the curio shop, but not as cashier. They tried that, but money confounds him; twenties are much the same as ones. It's easy for him to foul up, and for people to cheat him. What he's good at is dusting the old pine shelves and the merchandise, replacing the stock — stalagmite-shaped salt and pepper shakers, cutaway log slices laminated with pictures of the Azure Grotto and Bagnell Dam up by the Lake of the Ozarks. Old-fashioned souvenirs they buy from out-of-date companies. O-K Goods. Golly Notions. The only problem is when he occasionally takes too good care of things, gets on a dusting jag and polishes everything twice through. Or loses sight of the point and yanks a souvenir out of a customer's hands, placing it back on its shelf, just so, where it belongs. He always has such a look of righteousness afterward, a job well done.

Coming into the shop now, she finds him in another mode, sitting on a high stool in the corner, the lights off in the back of his eyes. He brightens slowly when he sees her, as though he's on a rheostat. She worries that when no one is around, William waits in this deactivated state — for whomever, but especially for her.

She thinks about Willie and the coming baby. In some ways he may be great with the kid. He loves repeating things, can play the simplest games for hours. That's the up side. He can also be full of mischief. When they were little, he used to enjoy coming up behind Jesse on the stairs and giving her a little push. She'll just have to keep an eye out.

"Hungry?" Jesse says, smoothing back his damp hair.

He shakes his head.

"I know it's hot. Come anyway. Have some lemonade, at least."

She takes his hand to pull him off the stool, but he begins shaking it hello. A joke he enjoys.

"Let's hit the bunker," Neal says, back in the kitchen, stacking bologna sandwiches on a plate. It's so humid the white bread triangles bend limply over his fingers as he picks them up. Jesse hands William a stack of paper cups and the lemonade pitcher. She brings a bag of barbecue chips, and the three of them go into the big back bedroom.

She and Neal used to beat the heat by spending the worst nights sleeping in the cave on camp cots they would clatter down the steps, bundling themselves against the damp in cotton blankets, holding hands across the gap between the frames. Drifting into sleeps kept restless by light moans in their middle ears or stirrings in their cerebral cortexes or chills passing through their marrow — excitations caused by the nocturnal sighing, the subterranean exhalations, of the cave.

They don't do this now that Willie lives with them. He likes open spaces; even windowless rooms agitate him. One time years ago they brought him down into the cave, and he looked around in a wild, ratchety way, pivoting his head like an insect, and began slapping his hands against the outside of his thighs and making sounds that fell just shy of words. It was awful to watch. Jesse brought him up and out, calmed him down some with a ride behind her on the power mower, letting the slow circling and the wet green smell massage him. For the most part now, he pretends the cave doesn't exist.

After the first few days of this spell of heat, Neal tricked up this room — the only one in the house with an air conditioner — as a survival shelter, bringing in the TV and VCR on their castored cart, sofa pillows to prop at the head of the bed, lawn chairs to flip open at its foot. Now the three of them chill out in here and pass their evenings in the wide world of cable.

William likes the home shopping channels best. He thinks the announcers are "nice" and wants to buy everything. Jesse thinks that if the retarded had credit cards, they'd have houses piled to the ceilings with air deionizers and Cubic Zirconia tennis bracelets. Neal finesses through the high-numbered stations to get to "Love Connection." At the moment, Chuck Woolery is laughing and shaking his head in disbelief at a contestant, a thin guy with old-fashioned glasses and a shirt buttoned at the collar. He looks a little like Buddy Holly.

"This guy is so pathetic," Neal says. "He rented a limo to pick her up for the date. These guys should talk to me. They should call me first. I'm great with women."

"You haven't had any opportunity to be great with

women," Jesse points out. "First you were shy, then you met me."

"Well, I'm great with you."

When they met, Jesse was just back from Mexico City, looking to fill in the several suddenly open hours a day during which it was no longer necessary to be in water. What she did instead was pace, mostly inside herself. She would spend nights out on the sleeping porch of her mother's house, listening to the willow branches rustling like satin drapes. Lying on her back, looking out through the old bowed screens at the phosphorescent sky, longing for dawn, and for event.

Neal walked calmly into the middle of this, offering a way out. He didn't expect her to balance forever on some peak of greatness, or leap to some next peak. He thought it was fine for her just to fall and let him catch her. (Years later, when she went to see "Cat People," in the middle of the scene where John Heard, who's a zookeeper, ties Nastassja Kinski, who's secretly a panther, to the bed so he can make love to her without getting killed, Neal, who was sitting next to Jesse eating popcorn, tugged at her sleeve with buttery fingers and said, "That's how I felt when we were starting off.")

He takes things the way they come, which has kept him a contented person all the time Jesse has known him. And now their situation offers even more to be content with. The cave's a modest moneymaker, the baby's on the way. He tells Jesse he dreams all the time now of catching plump, rainbow-silvered fish. "Sometimes I don't even have a rod and reel. They just jump up into the boat."

He has worked softly on Jesse over the years, trying to

persuade her to his contented point of view, but all he has really been able to do is to put a layer of soundproofing between her and whatever it is she has always been listening for. If she is alone and quiet and the phone rings, it explodes inside her like a starter's pistol. For almost her whole life, ringing phones, mail carriers' sacks, telegram offices, have held too much promise, elevated her expectations in a way she can't account for. She can't say what the call is that she's waiting for, what is in the letter.

They started trying to have kids around the same time all their friends did. But it didn't happen. Jesse thought maybe her mother had been right in all her grim predictions about swim training, that her body was now ruined for all standard female purposes. That missing all those periods had thrown her permanently out of whack.

Somewhere into the third year of trying, she and Neal stopped talking about the possibility so much, and moved into an alternative version of married life which quickly filled up with him running the cave and Jesse taking her real estate license. They have a fairly lively social life — Friday night fish fries over at the VFW, Saturday nights playing cards with Claude and Laurel Owen. Roasting a chicken or two on Sunday afternoons for one or another combination of her and Neal's families.

It is the chickens, more than almost anything else, that have become markers of passing time for Jesse. Every time she pulls one out of the plastic sack and begins washing it off and wrestling out the giblets, settling it slippery in the Pyrex dish, banking it with equally pale and translucent wedges of onion, she thinks, how many chickens does this make? For how many chickens has she been here, standing in place?

Sometimes she's amazed she has been with Neal more than twenty years. It seems more should have happened. When she hears couples say they've been through a lot together, that they're survivors, Jesse realizes she and Neal haven't had to survive much of anything other than his attack of kidney stones and the time she slipped on a patch of ice and put her hand through the storm door. And of course they've had to adjust to taking on William, which they did a few years back on account of him getting to be too much for Jesse's mother. But for the most part when she looks back on the long series of days she and Neal have shared, they look much the same.

But now, suddenly, there is change everywhere on the horizon. Sometime last winter — after years and years of having pretty much dismissed the likelihood of having any kid around besides Willie — Jesse suddenly began to feel different from any way she had ever felt before. Heavier, and at the same time more buoyant. She knew right off, and began counting in months.

They know from the test it's a girl. They got a book of names, but most of them seemed too pale and ordinary. For this surprising baby, they needed an exceptional name — to launch her into life with a little something extra. Bathsheba. Désirée. Jasmine. They squabbled over these for a while, then instantly agreed on Olivia, and that was that.

During the commercial, Neal pulls from his T-shirt pocket a soft plastic miniature slice of pizza with a hook dangling from its point. "Fred Otto gave me this lure. He says it pulls in the bass like crazy. Who'd think so, but why not I guess? Everybody else likes pizza, why not fish?"

"I think I've got another Fenny's Lake place sold," Jesse

tells him while William inspects the lure. "To Alice Avery. The Inn's such a big success that she's being run out of her own home. Wants a place further back up the lake, and I've got just the property for her. My red-letter day is right around the corner, I can feel it."

When "Love Connection" is over, they punch in a tape of the last two days' episodes of "M.D./R.N.," a soap opera they're addicted to. Or more correctly, a soap Jesse is addicted to and has dragged Neal and Willie along with her.

"Why's she leaving Rick?" Neal says when Sarah, head of the hospital pharmacy (and secret diet pill abuser), has hurled a toaster across her kitchen and stormed out with such vehemence that the flimsy prop wall wobbles. Neal only half watches this show and so often loses plot lines.

"He was selling crack to her little sister. Plus she suspects he's mixed up with those Asian gangsters. I myself think it's because their white-bread viewers don't like the guy who plays him. He has this tufting hair on his shoulders that shows in the make-out scenes. They're probably going to write in someone new for her. Someone just as rotten, but less furry."

"Which one's her sister?"

Jesse puts a silencing hand on his thigh. "Here's the good part," she says.

Rhonda, the sexy, wicked intensive care nurse is being interrogated by some cops. She's in her nurse hat even though they're at the police station. In all the other episodes for the past couple of weeks, Rhonda has been busy trying to kick over her traces after blowing away Stephen Poole, the hunky heart surgeon, who casually decided he wasn't going to leave his wealthy wife after all. When Rhonda gave him her ultimatum — Rhonda or his wife — he laughed. Big mistake.

Jesse loves Rhonda. At first she thought it was because the character is so outrageously ruthless, and then for another while she thought it was because the actress who plays her is so good, but then one day the truth just zapped her. In some small but significant way — something about her eyes, something lit up at the back of them, as though she's in on a secret — Rhonda is eerily reminiscent of Marty Finch.

By the time the second episode is over, Jesse feels cabin fever pressing in on them.

Neal, who can read her moods as though they are weather, says, "Why don't we go into town and get some ice cream at the Thirty-one Flavors?"

"You two go on without me," Jesse says. "I might just go for a little walk. Get the kinks out of my legs." She's finding that being pregnant is great for getting her out of almost anything she doesn't feel like doing.

"Supercuts?" William says, his voice giggly with hope.

"Hunh?" says Neal, dragging his attention off a commercial featuring a woman trying to lure a business-suited guy back into bed with how great she smells.

Jesse scissors two fingers across the top of Willie's hair.

"Sure," Neal says, and shrugs. "Why not?"

They try to hold these cuts down to once a month, but if Willie gets pitiful about it, Jesse lets him go sooner. It's only ten dollars, and it makes him so happy. He'd go every day if it was left to him. He has a crush on Darlene, one of the beauticians there, a tiny girl with haggard hair that looks like it has a heavy past separate from her own.

Jesse traces her bottom lip with the side of her thumb,

thinking. What she is thinking in particular at this moment is that the Supercuts is in a shopping plaza farther on from the 31 Flavors. And, if Willie gets a haircut, what with having to wait for Darlene, who's popular, they won't be back for over an hour. Which would give her time to drive out and meet Wayne Banks for fifteen minutes.

She waits at the window, watching them disappear down the long drive, Willie wrapped tight around Neal on the motorcycle as they set off for Highway 4 toward town. She rushes into the bathroom and puts on mascara, then a dab of concealer on the right-angle scar along her jaw, hits herself with a shot of Jontue, and pulls on a clean shirt and maternity jeans. She takes the Bronco and heads out in the opposite direction, toward Maple Lanes. It's Wednesday, Wayne's league night.

She knows every possible detail of his schedule. She has his time all mapped out on the inside of the cover of her Re/Max appointment book. This is essential. She can't have any life with him, can't even have dates or assignations. She can only find him when she can, and to do that she has to know where he is at any moment that might become a possible meeting moment. Sometimes, even when she can't get to him, she suddenly has to anyway. One time, last week, she was so suddenly flooded with the need to connect with him that she pulled over to a mailbox, left the motor running, and jumped out before she realized it wouldn't do. It would have to be a pay phone.

Everything works out tonight. It's like they are both inside the same oiled watchworks. His league isn't up yet when she gets there; he's just hanging out in the bar in his brown UPS pants and a short-sleeved black shirt with gold piping on the pocket and BLOCK ANIMAL HOSPITAL in satin letters sewn on the back.

He has just cracked a joke. She can tell from the even level of laughing from the guys around him, and the fact that he's not laughing, only looking vaguely accomplished and pulling on a beer. When Jesse comes through the front glass door, his lips go slack around the end of the bottle, and he nods almost imperceptibly to indicate he sees her. She gets change from Lonnie Powell, who weighs three hundred pounds and nearly fills the round booth from which he schedules lanes and rents shoes and balls.

Jesse uses two of the quarters to buy a Snickers, which she unwraps and eats as she walks around back to the Bronco, parked at the farthest reaches of the gravel lot. She gets into the back seat and waits behind the tinted glass, with the door open for Wayne, who follows in a few minutes, climbing in next to her. He unsnaps the clip at the base of her neck, freeing her hair. He is kneeling on the seat over her, like a paramedic with a patient in crisis.

"Oh, babe," he says, and Jesse feels like she's made of blue neon, the pulse of a jukebox. She pulls away the collar of his shirt and touches the protruding bone at the base of his neck, inhales his smell, a mix of sweat and Aramis.

It is three months now since she and Wayne started up. She had gone out to the airstrip in Bedelia with a pickup slip for a carton of T-shirts printed with Pratt's Caverns under a picture of the cave's stalactite xylophone. Wayne is the new local UPS guy, among other things. He's building a lively business around a light plane. He runs freight, dusts crops. This summer, he's been dragging advertising banners over the beach at the state park. Wayne is twenty-six, and life's an adventure as far as he's concerned.

Even now that she is so quicksanded with him, now that she's subject to aches in her glands when thoughts of him sneak up on her — even now, she's not clear why she got into this in the first place. If someone had asked her who could steal her even a little away from Neal, she would have first said no one. If pressed, she would have said Dennis Quaid.

Wayne is nothing like Dennis Quaid; he's an extremely rural type of person. He's from Arkansas. He has been around a bit, though, in a hitchhikey way through the south and west, a summer in Europe. He has a hip look about him — a little ponytail and a pierced ear — but it doesn't mean much. Style tics he picked up at the state university in Columbia. He didn't even go to any classes, just hung out for a couple of semesters. He came back with a trunkful of novels and shoe boxes full of blues tapes. He thinks because he reads Jack Kerouac and plays Ornette Coleman up in the air that his spirit soars above the rest of the local population.

Wayne is the kind who leaves, or at least talks about leaving, all the time. He chews gum and has a twitch pulsing under his left eyelid. He walks around frazzled with expectation, looking toward doors and horizons, checking his watch, combing his hair in the reflection of store windows as he passes. He riles Jesse in all the old ways, along with some new ones.

On Friday she goes out to the airstrip to see him. He wants her to come up with him while he practices skywriting, a new feature he's planning to add to the advertising end of his business.

"I can't," she tells him as they sit together in the low grass at the side of the tarmac. "I can't put the baby through loop-de-loops."

"Stay and watch from here, then," he says. "You can correct my grammar." When she smiles, he drops his fingertips onto her lips in a rippling way, as if he is noodling piano keys. "Olivia's mother," he says.

From up in the sky he tries to tell her "hi" in trailing smoke, but he has been practicing for only a couple of weeks, and has a ways to go yet. He starts his "h" too late, and winds up with "ni."

Technically, they're not even lovers. They've only gone so far as kissing. This makes it much worse. If she weren't pregnant, and they were sleeping together, having matinees in a room out at the Mona Lisa Motel, which has Jacuzzis in the bathrooms and advertises a "4-Hr Nap Rate," she could put this down as an affair and manage the guilt as best she could.

But this seems to be truly gruesome love. She feels yanked out of her ground, shaken up. Made stupid. Today for instance, she told Neal she was going to Dr. Ruben's for a prenatal checkup. At dinner, he'll ask how it went, and so on the way home, she'll have to pull over to the side of the road and read up on what is supposed to be happening in the seventh month. And then, next week, when she really does have an appointment with Ruben, she'll have to tell Neal she's going to the dentist, and then brush with baking soda in a gas station rest room so her teeth will look polished up when she gets back.

Sometimes it's even worse. One night she told Neal she was going to the 7-Eleven for dishwashing liquid, and then used the pay phone in the parking lot to call Wayne at home (he lives with a roommate) and persuade him to meet her on the bluff by Red Arrow Road. All this — the rushing and overthought plans so crucial to deceit — for ten minutes of kissing him in the dark, in the orange dash lights of the Bronco, like astronaut lovers.

She tries to keep the rest of her life as sensible as possible, as though this will serve as a counterweight to her secret madness. She makes lists of errands so she can run them in an efficient order. She has gone back to clipping coupons, something she hasn't done since the early, earnest days of her marriage. She logs all her appointments in her Re/Max daybook and works hard at being on time for them. It is in this spirit that she's doing 80 Saturday morning when she passes the 45 speed limit sign at the edge of New Jerusalem and gets pulled over by Dell Potter, who when they were growing up used to have the biggest collection of comic books in the neighborhood. Now he works for the highway patrol.

"Oh, Dell," Jesse says, getting out of her car in the strobe flash of his blue light.

"Jesse, you've got to stop driving like a yahoo. You're a pregnant lady."

"My mind was on this big sale I'm closing in on, so please don't go all police on me, will you?"

"Herbert told me he had to pull you over a few weeks ago."

She just gives him a friendly stare-down. They both know there's no way in hell he's going to write her a ticket.

While they stand there silently negotiating, Earl and Thelma Thompson roar by on their Harley, which is nearly as large as a car and painted candy apple red and blaring out from its radio one of those songs from the Christian station which sound like bland love songs, then turn out, a ways in, to be about Jesus. Too much friendliness with Earl and Thelma is an invitation to get proselytized, and so Dell just nods at them and Jesse waves, both in minimal ways. And Jesse begins singing, but low and without moving her lips, "I'll be riding into Heaven on my Harley," which is a pretty stupid joke, but it cracks Dell up, as though they're in church. When he straightens out, he says, "I'll let you off this once." It's what he has to say.

"Dell," she puts a hand on his arm at the bicep, "will you keep your fingers crossed for me? I think I'm going to sell Alice Avery another house. She's gotten too big for her britches over at the Inn, wants a place just for herself back up on the lake."

"That Skeeters is the best thing to happen around here in quite some time," he says.

"I haven't been yet," Jesse says. "I must be the last person in town."

"Have the pumpkin ravioli," he says over his shoulder as he goes back to his car. The radio is sputtering out a message. He reaches in and pulls out the microphone and tells it "Car Two," and waves Jesse on.

Jesse has been selling real estate around the tri-town area — New Jerusalem, Bedelia and Clay Center — since she got her license a dozen years ago. Until recently, this meant putting newlyweds and empty nesters into smaller places, everyone else into bigger ones, reshuffling the already-there population. Now though, there is the whole wild card of Fenny's Lake, a resort stretch ten miles out of town, popular in the twenties and thirties, done in by the Depression, and already long since fallen into disregard and disrepair by the time Jesse was in high school.

Back then the beach had been reclaimed by mosquito-filled marsh grass, the cottages mostly abandoned, except on summer nights when they filled up with vaporous residents—couples whose presence was manifest only through low moans and flashlight glow, thin wisps of transistorized music. And through their kicked-over traces — used sheepskin condoms and empty pints of Southern Comfort.

In the past couple of years, though, these cottages have piqued the interest of artistic types from St. Louis and Kansas City, who have been buying them cheap, knocking out walls and putting holes in the roofs and fitting them up as studios for painting and throwing pots and even writing music. The general population is suspicious of, and excited by these invaders, as though they've been landing at night outside town, in saucers. Even the cultured types — members of the Palette Club and the Bookmark Society — are withholding final judgment until they get a better look, but they can't stop looking.

Jesse has already sold four lake houses, including the largest, the old Murchison eyesore. The woman who bought this, Alice Avery, is about Jesse's age. She was a chef at a restaurant in Kansas City and now has revamped the sagging old Victorian into the Fenny Inn, with four guest rooms on the second floor, a sauna in the basement (where rumor has it guests get naked, although Jesse has never heard anybody who could vouch for this firsthand), and a gourmet restaurant, Skeeters, in what used to be the living and dining rooms.

Jesse never thought this sort of thing would go over around here, where people like large hunks of cooked-to-gray meat at the center of their meals and recognizable, soft vegetables at the outskirts. But she was wrong. You have to call two weeks ahead to get into Skeeters and eat Alice Avery's rare duck breasts and blackened shrimp and salads that have flower petals in them. The other night Jesse saw

Chief and Mrs. Purdy going in with the Eldermans, all dressed up and rustling along up the brick walk with hilarity and anticipation. It's like everyone has just been waiting for Alice to show up.

Jesse stands a little in awe of Alice's powers to overcome the resistance to change which is practically the cornerstone of New Jerusalem. At first she was envious, wondered why she hadn't thought of all this. But really, it had to come from an outsider to seem truly new, fresh.

"I think maybe Alice Avery's restaurant makes everyone feel there's a party," she told Neal the other day. "And they're tickled to be asked. De-fucking-lighted."

"Do you want to go sometime?" he said. "See what all the fuss is about?"

"I suppose I must."

When she meets Alice at the Re/Max office this morning to pick up keys for the Fenny's Lake place, Jesse turns from the peg board to see Alice looking back at her too hard.

"I've been thinking about this for a while, trying to remember where I've seen you before. Pratt, Pratt, Pratt, I'd say, but I couldn't get a bell to ring. Then somebody — Persis Goudy, I think it was — referred to you by your maiden name, and bingo! You're Jesse Austin."

Jesse laughs, purely astonished. "This never happens." It's true. Nobody ever recognizes her. The biggest reason is that, in her moment of glory, Jesse was facedown in several feet of water, shaved and suited and capped and goggled. In the news photos she was still wet and smiling too largely, her hair (short then) finger-combed off her face. Even her mother asked, "Which one is you, anyway?"

Alice pushes Jesse into embarrassment by rushing on

with a flurry of admiration. What a thrill it is. "I was just a decent club swimmer myself, so you can imagine. Getting to meet one of my idols, after all these years."

Jesse tries to see the swimmer inside Alice, who is now quite padded, presumably in all that good cooking of hers.

"I still remember you in that little film about the Olympics they showed us at school . . ." Alice says.

"The Courage to Try," Jesse fills in, and is immediately embarrassed for the film. Worse, for having its title right there on the tip of her tongue.

"What ever happened to" — Jesse is hoping she won't remember, but it takes Alice only a flash second to pull up the name — "Marty Finch? What a swimmer. Everybody up on the blocks against her must've had chills. You must've hated her."

In lieu of speaking, which is quite impossible in this moment, Jesse gets up and pours herself a mug of burnt sludge from the Mr. Coffee, which has been turned off since the previous morning. Then she has to pretend it is hot and drinkable, but at the same time can't offer any to Alice, who sees what's going on anyway, and says, "I'm sorry. I often trip over other people's wires, even when they've considerately laid them underground." Then she pushes open the screen door. "What say we have a look at that house?"

On their way out to the lake, Alice says, "So, do you still swim?"

"Nah," Jesse says. An all-purpose lie.

"There's a screened-in porch off the back bedroom," she tells Alice as they stand in the empty living room of this house on the nearly deserted north shore of the lake. The house Alice is thinking of buying for herself. If she does, it will have to stop being the house Jesse and Wayne use as a rendezvous point when they have more than an hour to spare with each other. Where they sit on the weathered boards of the porch floor, Wayne propped against the wall, Jesse leaning back into him as if he's a human chair. He lifts her hair and drags his lips, which are fat and flat at the same time, like Mick Jagger's, across the back of her neck.

They do so little. Their connection seems so inconsequential once Jesse is away from it. By the time she gets home again, she often can't remember what it was they talked about.

"If I knocked out this wall," Alice is saying, rapping the one dividing the bedroom from the porch, "I'd have a tree house to sleep in."

"You might get a little spooked out here at night all by yourself. This far out, you're a ways from your next neighbor." Jesse prides herself on being an ethical broker, not just selling someone a house, but the right house.

"I won't be alone," she says. "A friend's moving down from Kansas City."

"Ah," Jesse says, and pauses so long in her speculation on Alice's personal life that Alice laughs.

"You're subtle. I'll say that for you."

"You mean how I didn't swallow my gum? I know. I'm smooth." Jesse yanks open a stuck door she doesn't remember and pokes her head into a cedar closet. "You must really like it here," she says to Alice. "To be sinking all these roots."

"I think the part I like *is* the roots. I've moved . . . I think six times in the past ten years or so. One reason or another," she says, lifting a hand, waving away the bother of further explanation. "Letting things go as I went, lightening my load. Now I'm practically a Berber — just my tent, my pot and my goat. I'd like to stop awhile. Add a cup and a plate. Hang a picture. You have to understand this. I mean, it's the impulse you've followed yourself."

"Because I've stayed here?" Jesse says, then shakes her head. "That's a complicated business, not a simple one. People like you—"

"Please. Don't say 'people like me.' "

"I'm sorry. You, then. You come out from the city and think small means simple when all it really means is complicated in a smaller space. Which sometimes adds to the complication."

In the middle of saying this, Jesse's regular thoughts are interrupted by a special bulletin from Wayne. First she thinks it's just some kind of free association, that when she thinks "complication," images of Wayne instantly follow. Then she realizes it's his smell, that there are trace elements of Aramis in the air. Then she catches Alice's straight-on gaze shifting to something just beyond Jesse's shoulder. Jesse turns to see what she is looking at.

He is standing breathless in the doorway. He must have seen the Bronco parked outside and thought. . . . He has already seen his mistake, but it's too late. Anyone looking at him, looking at Jesse, would know. Alice Avery could be a post, and know.

"My friend Wayne," Jesse says. No point pretending he's the meter reader.

He nods. "I was just passing by. Saw your truck. I got a shipment for you. Salt and pepper shakers." He says this and they listen and no one believes a word. The worst of it is that Jesse can't even feel fear. Her only emotion at the moment is a terrible sadness that because she has to show

Alice the rest of the house, she won't be able to have this
time with Wayne. She has lost one of their finite number of
times left together.

That night, Laurel and Claude Owen are by to play Sheepshead. Laurel is Jesse's oldest friend, which is to say they
grew up on the same block and have known each other
since before kindergarten, since before everything. Claude
is originally from Wisconsin, where they play this great
stupid card game — with tens higher than kings, and
queens and jacks and all diamonds as trumps, and part-
nerships that split up and re-form hand by hand — and he
has taught them all. They're hooked on it now, there's no
prying them away from it. They play over here most of the
time, so Claude and Laurel can hire a sitter and get away
from their kids for a few hours.

Neal has decided to be the picker this hand and is looking over what he got in the blind, figuring out which four
cards he will bury for points. This will take forever. He is
an impossibly deliberate player.

"I can fold out the sofa bed for you guys," Jesse says to
Claude and Laurel. "In case we don't get to play this hand
until morning."

"I only play more brilliantly under this kind of pressure,"
Neal says. He is a mauerer, meaning he never picks unless
he is holding the hand of the century. And now he's grin-
ning at whatever bonus he got in the blind. Trying to rattle
everyone.

"Are you going to Peg's shower Tuesday?" Laurel says.
Jesse rolls her eyes.

"Oh, come on. It'll be fun. They're supposed to have a
male stripper come and surprise her."

"I already got Peggy Palumbo a toaster oven for her first marriage, even though I knew Greg was already sleeping around even before the wedding. Now I'm going to have to shell out for sexy lingerie she can wear on her honeymoon with Rich Coombs, who you just know has long yellow toenails and pee stains on his Jockey shorts. Peg doesn't have to wear black lace to get him turned on. All she has to do is show up. Actually, she could probably just phone in."

"Sometimes I'm sorry I couldn't have been born a woman," Neal says, not looking up from his hand, "and instead of sports talk and sexual bragging, I could have deep, sensitive conversations with my girlfriends."

"Yeah," Claude says. "Bonding conversations."

It was Laurel who fixed up Jesse and Neal in the first place. He is Laurel's cousin. Jesse didn't know him in high school. He grew up in Haney's Corners, came to New Jerusalem to take on the cave, which his family had started him off with instead of one of their carnivals — hotbeds of trouble.

The three of them, Laurel and Jesse and Neal, went together over to Ted Gates's Wound Day party. Before he came to work at the Texaco station, Ted had quit high school and signed up with the army and got shipped to Vietnam for about ten minutes, one of which was an extremely bad minute of getting shot in fifteen or so places. To commemorate this tiny piece of stopped time, he would celebrate every year by laying in several pony kegs, pinning his Purple Heart to his T-shirt, and letting anyone who wanted see his scars. "For free."

Jesse liked Neal straightaway. She was practically sold on him by the time they left the party. They'd spent most of it talking, drinking paper cups of foamy beer, sitting side by side on a rusty swing set left behind by whoever had Ted's house before him. On the way home, Jesse hugged Laurel and, out of Neal's earshot, told her he was the nicest thing anyone had ever done for her.

She had never met anyone who was more of a sure thing, sure to stay put in her life now that he'd walked through its door. Now she could unhook her hopes from lost love. Now she didn't have to go looking for a future.

Laurel was the one who went on to a big future, first to college, where she met Claude. When they graduated, they got married and began moving around a lot so Claude could set up QwikLube franchises. They've lived in Flint, Michigan, in Calgary up in Canada, in Belgium, and for a year in Abu Dhabi. Each of their four kids was born in a different place. Now Claude has been transferred to a territory covering the middle southern states, and is working out of New Jerusalem to make Laurel happy. She wanted to come home for a while to be near her mother and sisters. She and Claude have been back less than a year, and don't really know how long they'll be staying before he gets sent off somewhere else.

When Jesse thinks about Laurel, it's mostly as she used to be, in grade school and junior high and high school. When she was so shy about her skinny legs, she tried to get Miss Thorpe, the gym teacher, to let her play basketball in her raincoat. When she brought strange hot lunches to school, mysterious murky soups and stews packed into a widemouthed thermos by her mother, who is a strict vegetarian. Jesse remembers the thick slices of dense, dark bread Laurel would eat silently while everyone else at the table had steam table cheeseburgers and little glass cups of pudding with a rubbery skin on top.

Jesse thinks she probably remembers Laurel's younger self better than Laurel does. Living her whole life in this one place sometimes makes Jesse feel as though she is holding the heavy scrapbook of her friends' pasts, while they're able to move streamlined into unfurnished presents. It's an extension of the feeling she used to have as a girl standing in the Goudys' pasture, her Schwinn propped against her hip as she'd watch the long-distance trains shrilling past, on their way from here to there, New Jerusalem being neither.

She missed the one fast chance she had to slip out — when Tom Bellini came first to Mexico City scouting the U.S. women's team, then down to Missouri later that summer, trying to persuade Jesse to endorse a signature racing suit for his sportswear company. He had a mock-up with him, designed like a tennis sweater, only with the colors reversed — navy with a V-neck bordered in white and maroon. He wanted her to sign her name, to be replicated on thousands of these suits, and then go on a ten-city promotion tour with him. She couldn't tell if, along with this offer, he was flirting with her.

But by then she was wanting to cut free from swimming, which seemed to have taken so much from her and given so little back, really. Plus she had just started up with Neal, who stood solid and unblinking in front of her, holding her hand lest she drift back up into the ozone, offering her the alternative of himself.

The night is so hot, it really doesn't seem like any relief from the day. Neal has offered to set up the card table down in the cave, where it is always cool no matter what, but Claude is with Willie on this one. The caverns creep him out. And so the four of them are sitting around the dining room table between two roaring box fans, drinking beer out of sweating bottles and Cokes poured over lots of ice, and eating Cheetos, which Claude says is the official snack food of Sheepshead. They've got the oldies station on the radio in the living room. Little Eva is singing, "So come on, come on, *do* . . . the Loco-Motion with me."

"I like imagining this scene," Claude says as long as they're waiting forever for Neal to get his plan of attack together. "There's this party. Middle-aged folks, but still rockers. Like us. And there's this black woman there and she's just one of the bunch, there with her husband. They have kids. She works for the phone company. She's nobody, like everybody. And then this song comes on and she smiles and she says, 'That's me. I was Little Eva.' "

Jesse doesn't say anything. No one else draws the analogy between one-hit rock stars and one-race swimmers, members of the same sorority of failed expectation.

She looks off into the living room, where Willie is doing a sulky dance by himself. He has been in there, muttering and brooding around the floor for most of an hour. He knows, because Claude stupidly told him once, that there is a five-handed version of Sheepshead that could include him.

Jesse is hugely uncomfortable. This just started lately. She can't find a sitting position that doesn't ache somewhere. She has terrible gas. She feels as though she is carrying three squabbling toddlers instead of the one tiny girl Dr. Ruben assures her is the sole occupant of her uterus.

Neal takes the first four tricks of the hand, which does not bode well for their chances against him. Trumps are falling like dead leaves. He's whistling "We're in the Money," curling a frizzy lock of beard around his index finger, and looking heavenward. He almost never takes a hand. Either he's too timid to be picker, or he has some failure of nerve along the way and trips on his game plan. Jesse doesn't care that his winning the hand will put her score in the hole. It's still fun watching him take tricks with various flourishes.

The phone rings into the last two of these tricks.

"I've got a big nothing, so just lay them down for me any old way," she says, handing her cards to Laurel as she creaks up off the chair, as though being hoisted by an invisible winch. The closest extension is the wall phone in the kitchen. She picks up, and before she can even say hello, he's saying, "I love you. I'm crazy with it. I had to call. Don't be mad. Just say you're sorry I have the wrong number."

Jesse's a beat late.

"Say it."

"I think you have the wrong number."

She walks slowly back to the table. She should be furious. Instead she's thrilled.

"They wanted somebody else," she tells the others. *They*. Afraid to give him so much as a gender.

Sunday afternoon, she leaves the gift shop in the hands of Linda Mazur — an almost impossibly responsible and good-natured high school girl who is working for them this summer — while Jesse takes William swimming. She hasn't stopped, as she told Alice Avery, only taken swimming away from sidelong glances, stopwatch eyes, which is what she gets if she shows up at either of the pools she trained in here — the high school or the country club. Now she goes only with Willie, out to the old Tyler quarry. It's so far

from town and so enfolded in trees that it has been forgotten by one generation of rope swingers and inner tube
floaters and so, lost to a new one. For the several years
they've been coming here, she and Willie have had the
quarry to themselves.

Usually he loafs inside his tube while Jesse does languid
laps. Today they are both just flattened with relief to be
submerged away from the heat. Willie idles in his tire while
Jesse floats on a plastic blow-up raft, her hair drifting out
behind her, her belly a small island. After a while, he pad-
dles over.

"Will the baby come out soon?" He touches her stomach
lightly.

"September. It'll be cooler by then."

"A girl baby."

"Yes. Olivia. You'll like her."

"Maybe." He can be pretty cagey sometimes.

"Oh, Cowboy," she says. He bats her away with a hand
in the air. He pretends to hate (but really loves, she's sure)
this old, teasing name that goes back to when the family had
fantasies about what he'd be when he grew up. Back before
it became absolutely clear that he wouldn't.

She visors her eyes with her hand and watches him drift
away from her. He's splayed out across his inner tube, his
calves and arms submerged, his head thrown back over the
rubber, the crown grazing the water. His hair is red like
Jesse's, although fine and straight instead of coarse and
wavy, and there's much less of it now. She knows he frets
about this; she has caught him combing this way and that
in front of the bathroom mirror. Darlene at Supercuts sold
him some styling mousse, which puffs it up like a little
soufflé on top. He thinks this is an improvement.

He looks like a pink, freckled lily pad, the picture of contentment. All his life, people have been telling Jesse he might well be better off than everyone else, without the usual cares and woes, happy all the time. She hates this. She has never thought of his retardation as something that *is* him, but rather something that wraps and suppresses him. A too heavy overcoat that muffles the real Willie inside. And she thinks if you asked the inside Willie if he'd like to get out of the coat, even though it would mean dropping the protective layer, he'd jump at the chance.

Jesse wishes she could see in there. Sometimes this happens for a flash; she gets a glimpse. One time they were in the A & W lot. She had just ordered a couple of mugs over the speakerbox, then turned to ask if he wanted onion rings, too, and got stopped by his expression, which had taken on sharp, focused aspects of adulthood. For a split second he appeared full of thought and concerns, poised to say something. And then, the expression faded, his features slipped back into their usual state of guileless expectancy, as though life was just about to start happening for him.

"Don't you have anything more of Flannery O'Connor?" she says as she hears Vernon Moore coming down the fiction aisle toward her, his stiff khaki pants squeaking as he walks. He's a large man, a college linebacker easing into middle age with the shadow of his younger, more athletic self lingering around him uncomfortably now that his physicality is constrained between narrow aisles of soft-paged volumes. Jesse knows how he feels.

It's Monday. She is stopping at the library mostly to pick up detective novels for her godmother. Who is perfectly capable of getting them for herself, but likes the attention.

"There's a volume of her letters. I could get it through interloan if you want. Might take awhile is all."

Jesse shrugs. "I've probably got awhile."

Jesse reads in a self-improving way, a meandering program of acquisition she began years ago. She is working toward being well-read — filled with important quotes and stinging observations and hard, clear truths she will keep to herself. One of the most crucial aspects of this program is that Jesse's mother, who taught high school English for forty-three years until she retired this June and has an abiding belief in literature, shouldn't find out. She would only take it as tribute.

Jesse's secret is safe with Vernon. He is still an outsider here, one of the few black professionals in town. He's from St. Louis and is not very happy with this assignment. The state library system assigned him to this branch, inadvertently pressing a bit of affirmative action on New Jerusalem. In return, the town pays Vernon the sort of overwrought respect and politeness that amounts to ostracism.

"Here. I thought you might be interested in this," he says, handing her a book. It's new; she can tell by riffling the pages close to her face and inhaling, a pleasure held over from childhood. It's a biography of Amelia Earhart.

"I don't know, Vernon, biographies always depress me. I mean, you know, how they all end the same way."

"That's the point. You only munch novels and you get too hopeful a vision. Biographies bring you down. They're cautionary."

"But what's the caution?"

He holds out an open cellophane pack of Gummi Bears to her.

"Now," he says. "*Now* is what biographies whisper. Soon it will be too late."

She checks out the Earhart, along with a short stack of murder mysteries for Hallie. Although in real life Jesse's godmother is even-tempered and filled with good will toward nearly everyone, the books she most enjoys are stories of murderers with villainous hearts and grisly m.o.'s. Although Jesse has never read one of these books, she's getting pretty good at picking them.

She walks the two blocks to the Fricke Building, New Jerusalem's "skyscraper," where Hallie has had her business for more than forty years. A single room at the end of the hall on the fifth (and top) floor. Hand-painted letters on frosted glass:

HARPER METHOD
SCALP TREATMENTS
MISS H. BUTTS, OPERATOR

Hallie opened this parlor in the mid-forties, when the Method was in its heyday. Like most operators, she was a single lady, devoted to her clientele. Among the first was Jesse's father, who took the Method religiously.

It was one of his embarrassing (to Jesse) eccentricities, along with his unicycle, his rubber bathing cap, the black wool knee socks he wore with long bermudas. Even now, so many years after him, Jesse still sees him in this parlor, the ticking-striped drape over his shoulders. The Method is emblematic of all the oddball notions he was devoted to. But it is also important to Hallie, who, although she is cynical about everything else, has an unswerving, totally humorless belief in scalp hygienics. And so that she will have four regular customers rather than three, Jesse has pretended to be a late convert.

Jesse pushes open the humidity-swollen door. Inside, it's 1946. The trio of maroon vinyl and pocked chrome waiting chairs hug the wall, empty of waiters for some years now. The huge single window, framed in dark, over-varnished wood, is blocked by a giant floor fan slapping sluggishly at the dead air. Hallie, wearing her shiny white nylon uniform, although probably no one but Jesse will come by today, sits in the hydraulic client chair, sucking on a Pall Mall and reading *The Corpse Took a Taxi*. She looks up and smiles.

"My, my, what have we here, my little fix?" She crushes out her cigarette, gets up, and comes to look the books over.

"I couldn't remember if I've already brought you this one," Jesse says, picking up *Cause of Death: Blonde*.

Hallie shakes her head as she goes through the rest of the titles. "Nope. You did good. These are all fresh blood, new gore."

She sets the stack on one of the waiting chairs. When she straightens up, she looks at the wall clock, its second hand sweeping over a picture of a squat white jar of Harper Method ointment.

"Well now, isn't this just perfection? My two-thirty canceled," she says for form's sake. "If we get right down to it, I can probably squeeze you in. And," she stops to unclip Jesse's hair, rubbing a few ends between her professional fingers, "you do look as though you could use a treatment."

Jesse grabs onto the arms of the customer chair and lowers herself with some difficulty. She looks up at Hallie's arms, beefy from working over the scalps of three generations of heads. Now the skin hangs loose from the giant knots of muscle; she's still robust, but in a rickety way.

She shakes a can, and bran drifts down onto Jesse's hair. Then she picks up a wooden-backed, boar bristle brush and begins the punishing strokes. "You know the dead dentists?" she says, referring to the three tiny offices in a row on this floor. "Well, one actually died. This week. He was working all the way to the end, although thank goodness not on me. You should have seen that equipment."

"What?" Jesse says. "Pliers? A hand drill?"

"Close."

For a minute or two as Hallie gets her rhythm, there's just the thwapping of the fan blades and the brush, and the soft-shoe shush of her stepping around in the fallen bran. She stops a moment to tug a brochure out of the mirror frame and hand it to Jesse.

"Joy dropped it by. She says it's a terrific deal."

The pamphlet, its cover a collage of the Colosseum and the Trevi Fountain and the Sistine Chapel ceiling, advertises a ten-day excursion to Rome. "The Eternal City," Hallie calls it, having picked this up a few brochures back. She and Jesse have been planning a trip there since an afternoon years ago when they'd driven over to Hot Springs, Arkansas, to cruise the tourist traps. On a lark, they stopped in to consult an astrologer operating out of a red and gold storefront, two doors down from Animal I.Q., where for two dollars you could go inside and see a chicken peck out tunes on a tiny piano, four dogs sitting at a table playing cards.

The astrologer, Cecil Luster, told Hallie and Jesse they were spiritually linked. That this connection had been formed in ancient Rome, and that they would both eventually find their way back there. Once put into their heads, the very improbability of these notions ran a feather under their imaginations and has given them years of feeling mysteriously slipknotted to each other, and to an exotic place, an unknowable past.

"Do you think we'll ever really go?" Jesse says dreamily, ducking her head rhythmically under the brush strokes.

The case against them becoming footloose travelers is getting pretty strong. Aside from the Olympics and three Method conventions in Rochester, New York, the last of these in the early sixties, Hallie has not ventured much beyond Missouri and Arkansas in her sixty-five years. Neither she nor Jesse has been anywhere to speak of since Mexico City.

"Well, I've always felt a bit chafed here," Hallie says. "And I can get pretty riled up by television travel shows. They make it seem like rolling off a log to get from here to there — to wherever. But when I try to imagine actually going myself, actually pulling on my girdle and catching the Trailways out, all I can think of are all the possibilities for mistakes and embarrassment."

She sets the brush down, warms her palms by rubbing them up and down over her hips for a minute, then pulls a generous fingerful of ointment out of a large open jar and begins working it into Jesse's scalp.

"Like I forget one of my prescriptions. I'm all harebrained getting ready for the trip and leave it behind on the kitchen counter. Now I'm in a foreign place. Not someplace nice where I'm having myself a wonderful time. Just a kind of generic foreign place. And I have to find a drugstore, or whatever they have there that's like a drugstore. It turns out to be a place with bottles in the window, murky liquids, roots in jars of thick syrups. There's a dried hoof on the counter. And of course I don't know the language, so I have to pantomime my problem for the druggist. Something hideously embarrassing."

"Hemorrhoids," Jesse helps.

"Athlete's foot'd do."

"Well, we've got a reprieve from showing we can do it," Jesse says, patting her stomach. "We can't go until the baby can do without me for a while, or until she's old enough to bring along."

The old dial phone sitting on the glass cabinet of brushes and shampoos for sale rings, crashing into the sleepy atmosphere of the parlor.

"Never fails," Hallie says, holding up her greased hands. "Probably my three-thirty saying she'll be a little tardy." She grabs a towel and wipes her large hands roughly before picking up. Jesse can tell within seconds that this is a personal call, within a minute that it's Hallie's best friend, Jesse's mother.

"Too much bother," Hallie is saying. Jesse peers over her godmother's shiny hand. COFFEE is what she has written in childish block letters on a scratch pad. "Why don't I just get one of those big electric urns from the U-Rent?" Jesse sees this is one of the hundred details for the big party Hallie is throwing for Frances's combination sixty-fifth birthday and retirement from the public schools. Jesse will be on the guest list (she and her mother try to hold their breach beneath the notice of the town gossips), but she isn't being included in any of the planning.

When Hallie hangs up, she pulls a flat box from the bottom shelf of the glass counter, opens it, and offers Jesse a chocolate-covered apricot. She keeps these — a childhood favorite of Jesse's — around for whenever she stops by. Neither of them says anything for quite a while. Hallie dips up a bit more ointment and goes back to work on Jesse's scalp. Finally she says, "I'm trusting you to handle this information with a gracious touch."

"I'm the soul of graciousness," Jesse says, pushing herself up straighter in the chair, improving her moral posture.

"The fact is — and it's not all that flabbergasting if you really think about it — your mother has found herself a boyfriend."

"Oh my." Jesse tries to imagine this, tries to see her mother on a date. To Jesse's knowledge, Frances has never dated anyone except Jesse's father, and that was before Jesse was even around. In the more than twenty years since his death, she has continued a social life of Thursday-night bridge, a subscription to the Lakeside Players summer theater, and occasional lunches at the Tea Caddy with one or another of the same small retinue of friends she has had since she graduated from college and came back and slid into the middle of the middle class of New Jerusalem. Methodists as opposed to Episcopalians or Baptists.

Like many other wives she watched as her husband went into business, began to go bald, and read more and more of the newspaper, and developed firmer and firmer opinions on what he read, and then died sooner than anyone expected of cancer, liver problems, or a heart attack. In her case, the business was the drugstore on Willow, where Ray Austin dispensed medical advice as though he were an M.D. And his opinions became not just firmer, but more and more eccentric as time went on. By the time he died — way earlier than anyone would have expected, of a massive heart attack while he was playing the tuba in the Fourth of July parade — Jesse suspects her mother was exhausted with the effort of nearly twenty years of not being embarrassed by him. After that, she folded up her marital and sexual tents and settled into a social life among the widows, a full calendar of nothing, which nonetheless seemed to leave no room for "boyfriends."

"His name is Darrell," Hallie says, still serious, as though she's talking about someone dying rather than someone falling in love. "He plays with a rock band over at the Blue Light. They played at the church dance awhile back is how she met him. He's not who you'd expect. I just want you to be nice to her around this if you run into her."

"I'm always nice."

"In your heart you're always nice, but in your mouth there's sometimes just the tiniest touch of sarcasm."

"And this Darren will sorely provoke me."

"Darrell. Just remember, Frances is really happy about this."

"He has a giant wen," Jesse guesses. "On his nose. Or, no . . . wait. He wears a drool cup."

Usually she can draw Hallie in right off the bat, but today she can feel resistance tugging through her godmother's fingertips before Hallie caves in and says, "It's an extremely *small* hump."

They are quiet for a time, the silence filled with their thoughts.

"A boyfriend," Jesse finally says. "A rock and roller. I'd have thought she'd had enough of oddballs with Dad."

"Come on," Hallie says, picking up the hairbrush and tapping Jesse's head with the back of it. "This guy's a real Romeo, they say. Your old mother's kicking back."

"She's such a puzzle. I thought genes were supposed to give you some affinity, but . . . I mean aside from all the trouble between her and me, I've just never really felt whatever connection you're supposed to feel. Is that awful?" When Hallie doesn't reply, Jesse says, "I think the truth is you're secretly my mother. Like in those old movies — Olivia de Havilland, Barbara Stanwyck. You know. You were pregnant, but you weren't married and so what could you do? You slunk off to Jeff City to have me. And then you talked Mother into pretending I was hers and Dad's. And all these years you've had to love me — tragically — from afar."

"Sweetie, if I'd had you, it would've been only the second virgin birth in history." This is Hallie's standard line, that she has led a celibate life, is on a high shelf above the sexual shenanigans of everyone else. Jesse knows this can't be true, knows because she knows all the other pieces of Hallie. There's a blank spot, but its shape is not denial. There is simply something sitting in that spot that Hallie has, so far anyway, chosen not to reveal. It's okay. Jesse can wait.

Hallie is the only person she has had the nerve to tell about Wayne, which is to say Hallie is the only person it didn't take any nerve to tell. Her love for Jesse has always been unconditional. Jesse tests all the same. "Do you think less of me for this thing I'm doing?"

"Your timing's interesting, I'll say that."

"I've got to stop it. We almost got caught Saturday. Well, I suppose we *did* get caught. But it was by Alice Avery and she's so hip and all — "

"And has her own mysteries, they say. Eyebrows are up around here, waiting to see who she's bringing down to live with her. I think Opal Leach is putting a fax machine down at the post office so she can get the word out instantly." Hallie kneads Jesse's scalp for a few moments while suspended in reverie over something. Finally it comes out. "Goodness, I love the food that girl serves."

"I don't even know why I'm doing it," Jesse says. "It's so dead wrong. You know I love Neal with my soul. And now the baby. I just don't understand. It's like something's come over me."

"The devil," Hallie says in a phony, horror movie way.

"Could be. Honestly."

"We could take you up to Canaan. There's an old guy there who's a dowser, does exorcisms if pressed, I hear tell. Has something rigged up in the backyard. Electric currents and moonlight."

Jesse reaches up and, for a moment, holds on to Hallie's wrist.

"It's just that I want to, isn't it? It's just that plain. I want something I can't have but I want it anyway and so I'm taking it. And then, because I can't stand seeming so selfish, I chatter away about how wrong I know it is. As if that gives me points."

Neither of them says anything for a while, then Jesse says, "Are you going hard on me today? I feel like you're digging into my brain."

"Nope. This is just the standard treatment. I charge extra for the rough stuff."

But the next time she sees Wayne, Jesse just doesn't have the heart to lower any booms. She's over at his apartment in the middle of the afternoon. Both the Re/Max and UPS offices have little clock-face signs hanging on their doors, reading BACK AT 4.

He lives in a development out by the county airport. The apartments are regular on the inside, but the exteriors are fixed up in this fake English way. The whole place is called Hampshire Mews.

Wayne's roommate, Stan Feder, works at the Ace Hardware and is out of town at a paint seminar in St. Louis. This is a big opportunity for them. Wayne wanted to fix Jesse dinner, but she wasn't up to the amount of scheming that would have required. And so she's here for tea, or at least his idea of tea, which comes from movies and books, she guesses. The tea itself is instant. The sweets are Little Debbie snack cakes, arranged on a scratched plastic plate. He has also set out colored paper napkins. The apartment has central air, which adds a hum and a chill factor. Jesse has to borrow a sweatshirt as soon as she's through the door. Even though it's huge, the waistband cinches her stomach like a rubber band.

Wayne has Alberta Hunter on the CD player. Everything in this apartment is sprung, broken, and was already junk when it was new. Except his sound system, which cost more than his car.

He has a present for her, a robe. It's black satin, knee-length, with black lace lapels. She can tell from the Victoria's Secret box he went all the way up to the mall in Jefferson City to buy it.

"Happy birthday," he says. Her birthday is in March. "I don't mean for you to wear this now. It's for after."

She doesn't say anything.

"I can keep it here," he says.

She starts to cry.

"Don't say anything," he says when she still doesn't say anything.

He cuts a snack cake in two and puts a half on her plate,

then licks a dab of white filling off his thumb. "I know it's hard on you. I'm just thinking that maybe, after the baby comes . . ."

She puts her head in her hand, to stop the sentence. She already knows where it's going. His notion seems to be that being involved with someone who is a wife and mother will be less of a problem than being involved with a pregnant lady. She suspects he has hopes of then persuading her to leave Neal and New Jerusalem behind and go soaring off with him into skies above other places.

She can't imagine any of this. Even in the privacy of her mind, she never takes this any further than it actually goes. She holds it in a present tense of kissing in cars, listening to bluesy music, her being impossibly pregnant, him being impossibly young. This *is* what it is. She can't find any place on it where she can even pin a hope.

"Oh, excuse me," someone says. Jesse turns to find out the grocery cart that has just banged into her from behind is being driven by her mother. It's the express line and Jesse has her package of ground beef, carton of macaroni salad, and Summer's Bounty starter plate on the belt, ready to be expressed while she reads a tabloid borrowed from a nearby rack. Her mother has caught her at a good moment, looking for the cover story on the baby born with a tattoo on its arm.

"I'll have to make a citizen's arrest on you," Jesse says, nodding toward her mother's half-full cart, way over the TEN ITEMS OR LESS posted on the cardboard sign above the cash register, trying to put her on the defensive, usually the best way to begin a conversation with Frances.

"Wendy and I have an understanding," her mother says.

Wendy is the checkout girl, who still looks about thirteen despite having worked here for years.

Jesse is wishing she didn't have a ninety-nine-cent plastic plate on the belt next to her, and a tabloid in her hand. Two of her mother's most cherished beliefs about Jesse are that she is stuck just above the poverty and literacy lines.

"Hallie tells me you've gotten yourself a beau."

"Well, I am seeing someone."

Seeing someone. This has an amazing sound falling from her mother's lips — the foreign, metallic sound of a lunatic pronouncement, as though she's quoting a headline from the paper Jesse has just slid back into its rack. As though her mother is saying Elvis is alive and living with Natalie Wood in a gas station out in the Mojave Desert. Jesse hopes she's not looking amused.

"You might wipe that smirk off your face," her mother says as Wendy hands Jesse her change, as usual dropping the coins on top of the dollar bills so they slide onto the conveyor belt. Jesse picks up the change and stuffs it along with the folded money and the register tape into the back pocket of her jeans.

"Hey, I'm . . ." Jesse starts, not sure where she's going.

But her mother is already bustling her frozen entrees and skim milk and air deodorizer packs out of the cart, flashing Wendy a witheringly false smile, the one she thinks has made her so popular among "shop people" for years.

Jesse tries, against her better judgment, to break this deadlock. "I mean, I'd like to meet him," she says, pulling her mother's attention off Wendy, but with the smile intact.

"I'm sure you would."

Jesse waits just long enough to see that this is it, the

conversation has been closed, then tosses her keys high into
the air and catches them just above her head as she steps on
the rubber pad before the automatic door and heads out to
the parking lot.

"Alice?" Jesse asks a collegiate-looking guy who shuts down
a vacuum cleaner when she comes into the dining room. It's
early Thursday morning; she's bringing the contract for the
house over to the Fenny Inn.

"Kitchen," he says, pointing.

Jesse comes through the swinging door and, seeing Alice
in a long apron, laughs.

"What?" Alice says.

"You look just like a chef."

"Well, what'd you think?" She nods toward the leatherette Re/Max folder Jesse is holding. "Time to sign my
life away, eh? Have you had breakfast? Why don't you let
me fix you an omelette? I've given up hope of ever seeing
you in that dining room. Might as well feed you in my
kitchen."

There aren't any chairs, so Jesse hikes herself up onto a
wooden stool against the wall, activating an old place of
soreness just inside her right shoulder blade, left over from
some peculiarity of her stroke, something done wrong in an
infinitesimal way, but repeated a million times in all the
practice laps of her youth. The insult has never been quite
forgiven by the aggrieved muscle, which still kicks back
with an occasional reminder.

Alice pulls from a shelf over the black iron stove a
copper-bottomed pan, into which she smears what looks
like half a stick of butter. She cracks eggs one-handed into
a metal bowl, beats them with a wire whisk, shreds a minor
mountain of Swiss cheese onto a plate.

"I've got one of those hinged pans, does the job for you," Jesse says. "I suppose I'll have to hide it if you ever drop by. And my bacon bits. My seasoned salt. My entire recipe card file."

Alice, having finger-sifted the cheese onto the bubbling eggs, makes a little move with her wrist, which both flips the omelette over on itself and slips it to one side of the pan. When the omelette is done, she slides it onto a plate and hands it to Jesse, along with a fork and a napkin. She pours both of them large cups of coffee, and sets Jesse's on the windowsill next to her. Then she wipes her hands on a towel stuck in the waist of her apron and leans back against the big chopping block in the center of the room.

"You eat. I'll look at the papers." She opens the Re/Max folder Jesse has brought with her and scans the contract, pulls a fat fountain pen from a hidden breast pocket, and signs.

"This is the most delicious plate of eggs I've ever had," Jesse says. "I'm proud to sell a house to the person who made these eggs."

Alice smiles and says, "Good. Let's go swimming."

"I told you, I don't anymore."

"I don't know why, but I just don't believe that."

Jesse finishes the last of the omelette.

"Alice, I appreciate your cooking, and your buying this house, and I'd like you anyway, but I'm a different kind of person from you. This is a different place from where you come from. I have my husband and my godmother. My brother. I don't have many friends. You seem to find me so interesting and I think I'm plain as can be. Or maybe I'm a plain person who just looks interesting. A plain person with a few sticks of dynamite strapped to her chest. I can feel you've got all these questions for me. You tripped onto my big secret, which I hope you'll hold for me. But ordinarily, I don't share confidences. I hate the gossip around this place."

"*Tell* me about it," Alice says. "My lover's moving down at the end of the month and I can practically feel the phone receivers already lifted, all those itchy fingers poised above the push buttons."

"Maybe I'm being too hard ass?" Jesse says.

"I'm not taking offense, if that's what you're asking."

This seems like a good enough ending to the conversation, and so Jesse doesn't understand why she feels like it's a dangling loose end for the two blocks it takes her before she U-turns back and pulls up to the doorway of Alice's kitchen and hops out. "Well, come on," she says sticking her head inside, nodding toward the Bronco idling high outside in the lot.

At the lip of the quarry, as she and Alice pull off their clothes, Jesse, who has undressed in front of thousands of strangers in hundreds of locker rooms in her life, is suddenly, unexpectedly modest. She hangs her T-shirt on a peg of broken branch and covers her enlarged breasts with her hands as she turns back toward Alice. "No one's seen me big like this except my doctor and my husband."

Alice nods in fascination, watching Jesse pull her suit on over her swollen belly. "Yeah. Pregnant sure is something."

They drift around each other in the inner tubes. In a way, Jesse feels as though she is betraying Willie, bringing someone else out here.

"How can it stay so cold in this heat?" Alice says, dragging her fingertips through the blue-black water.

"Depth, I suppose. They used to say this quarry's so deep no one knows where its bottom is."

"How come you changed your mind? About bringing me here?"

"I don't know. I don't seem to *know* my own mind these days. I tell you I don't want you nosing around in my life, and then I bring you to my most closely held place."

"I don't want you to think I'm after your secrets. I'm not. I'm just looking for a way in."

"Then why do I keep feeling all these questions hanging around? The ones you ask, the ones I can hear even though you're not asking them?"

Alice doesn't say anything. Jesse tries to catch her expression, but she can't. The sun behind Alice puts her in eclipse.

"Why do you want to know what happened? You know. Down there."

"In Mexico City?"

"Yes."

"I don't know," Alice says. "I just think maybe that's the place to start."

Jesse abandons her tire, and for a while swims slow, strong laps back and forth across the quarry. Then dives under, coming up through the center of her inner tube, tilts her head back, dipping her hair in the water to get it off her face.

"Okay. That summer — 1968 — Marty came out of nowhere. They were calling her the Australian Water-Eating Machine. It was like one day she just crept up over the edge of my horizon and was all of a sudden my worst fear. I'd come out on top at the nationals in the hundred-meter free. My times were really strong going down to Mexico City.

58

Which should have given me all the confidence in the world. But it didn't.

"The rumors just kept drifting around. Marty Finch was a phantom, a pure natural. Of course, at world-class levels, even naturals have to work, but they still have attitude left over from when they didn't.

"I was seventeen, a hick from Missouri. I'd spent a few months in Florida, at Sea Breeze — you remember it? They'd been turning out winners like Buicks off the line. I was the latest. Mostly I got to Mexico City by being a grind — an infinity of endurance laps and sprint work. You can't know. They'd only pull me out when my back went blue."

"Huh?"

"You know, when my heart couldn't pump up enough blood. I was the little engine that could. I guess a lot of people thought I'd take my event, but no one would ever have called me a water-eating machine. That's what got to me, I think."

"And then you met her," Alice says, as though she is inside the story.

"Yes. I expected her to high-hat me, but right from the start, that first night at the international dinner, she came over to where I was sitting.

("Let's be friends," Jesse remembers Marty saying. "It'll be more fun.")

"Weren't you a little suspicious?" Alice says.

"I don't know. I was mostly curious as hell. I'd never known anyone like her. She was only eighteen, but she seemed to have already thought herself through, and then remade herself up entirely. I guess I got crushed out on her arrogance."

What Jesse can't find a way to say is this was the first time she'd ever fallen in love, that she hadn't been at all prepared for it, and certainly wouldn't have expected it to happen with her arch rival. But of course, looking back, it wasn't the least bit surprising really. Her whole adolescence had been measured out in laps — by stopwatches and pulse rates and protein grams. She had been compressed for so long inside such a tight little shell of discipline, like a grenade. Marty just pulled the pin.

" 'Don't you want to be bad?' she'd say."

"By *bad* . . . ?" Alice says.

"I didn't know," Jesse says, and laughs. "I sure wanted to find out, though. We began sneaking off. To town. To the roof at night."

Down to the showers after everyone else was asleep, is what she doesn't add.

"Once, we went out of the city, to visit this Mexican girl Marty knew. Serafina Somebody. She'd trained in Brisbane for a time under Marty's coach. Her swimming days were behind her by that time. Her parents had this huge white-white house on this green-green lawn. In the back, they'd put in a pool. For Serafina, I guess.

"Before lunch, Marty and I fooled around in the water. No room to race and so we just splashed, dunked each other. Fish-swished along the bottom. Playing tag, kind of." Jesse pauses, trying to make a depth check on the safety of this conversation. "And then Marty came all the way from the bottom of the diving end, sliding up under me. Our faces were about an inch apart, our bodies just not quite touching. You know."

Neither she nor Alice says anything for a stretched moment. The crickets, which run on high, day and night, in the overgrowth around the quarry, fill in the silence with their white noise, at the same time deafening and beneath notice.

It's Alice who speaks first. "Bet you had trouble eating that lunch."

Jesse feels herself flushing, the universal curse of red-heads. "On the way back to town," she says, now in a hurry to finish, "in this rattletrap old taxi, kicking up giant pillows of dust, we made fun of how Serafina talked to Marty: 'I think of you constantly all these years,' was what she'd said. We figured it must be a bad translation. Still, we started saying 'I think of you constantly' instead of 'hi.' Afterwards, it was how I began the letters I sent down to Australia."

"Which went unanswered," Alice says.

"How could you know?" Jesse says, turning suddenly inside her inner tube, making the rubber screech.

Alice shakes her head. "I don't know. I could smell treachery coming, I guess. It's easy now, now that it's a story. When you were going through it, it was life. Always much harder to get the plot line on."

"And of course," Jesse says in her own defense, "everything was moving so fast. Plus I wanted to take everything as a good sign, a lucky charm."

The scene in her imagination comes up white, and she's back down in the showers, late at night. She and Marty lying next to each other on a bed made of layers and layers of towels.

"Marty would get all confessional," she tells Alice, "which I tried to take as a sign of something. But there was something off, even about the confessions. Like everything else about her, they were a little too easy. She hated to swim, she told me. It was just her ticket. Out of Pemby, this desperate place on the edge of the bush.

"I was impressed that someone only a year older than I

was already had a plan. Me, I'd done almost no thinking about my future. I got into swimming because I'd been good at it right off, and because it was something my parents didn't understand. It got me a little away from them. I was a big star here in New Jerusalem, which seemed to me as big as anyone could possibly want to be. Marty had a larger oyster in mind. She was going to be in the movies. She thought she had the California look, figured she'd get parts in surfer movies."

"Didn't she have a TV show?" Alice says. "I remember reading something in one of those 'Where Are They Now?' articles."

"I saw that, too. Something about an underwater private eye. It was only on down there, I guess. I mean I never saw it."

"It can't have really been about an underwater detective, can it?" Alice says. The idea sets her off laughing. "I mean how many underwater crimes are there? Or underwater criminals, for that matter?"

Jesse smiles sheepishly. "Maybe I've got it wrong. Anyway, the actress stuff was all part of this grand plan of hers, and a big element in it — although of course we never talked about it — was that she had to take the gold. Which meant she had to beat me."

Jesse doesn't say that this is what she turns on. That the friendship was calculated, that the seduction was just a piece of the arithmetic.

Alice puts it together anyway. "And you're thinking that if you get someone infatuated with you, it's hard for them to maintain a true killer instinct, to really care about beating you anymore."

"Oh, I can't know that for sure," Jesse says. "It could as easily be true that Marty liked me well enough, and aside from that, simply got through a hundred meters that particular day three-tenths of a second faster than I did. It could be just that."

"But if she liked you well enough, why did she disappear?"

Jesse shakes her head. "It's all just stupid to even think about anymore. The times we made have long since been passed by the newer, faster girls they're making nowadays. What happened that afternoon is something no one even cares about anymore. Except me, and I'm tired of caring. Sometimes I even think I've made up most of Marty Finch, invented this big betrayal to transform my own plain loss into something complicated. For sure, I've changed her in my mind over these years. Aged her, made her more sophisticated. It's like I keep translating her into whatever I need to keep the anger going."

And the passion, she doesn't say.

"So I can keep pulling a charge off her. Touch the wire. Keep feeling the current twitch through my fingers," Jesse says, being almost completely candid, almost candidly complete. Holding back only a few things, colors mostly. The night-white light down in the showers, and the aquamarine.

"Here." Neal pulls Jesse gently by the shoulders, then points up. "Right there."

At first she can't see what he's talking about. He tamps the dead flashlight down on his open palm, and the batteries jostle into place, making a connection that throws a shot of light on the problem — a crack up near the highest part of the vault in the Azure Grotto.

"Do you think it means anything?" she says. "Anything important, I mean?"

"Don't know. We get to thinking of this as an attraction, our place of business, that it belongs to us. But it really belongs to nature. Nature's always going to have the last word on it."

"What're you going to do?"

He takes off his baseball cap and runs a hand around his forehead and temples, where sweat has gathered. "I'll call Tim Sutter up in Columbia in the geology department. See if he can come down here and have a look. In the meantime, we should probably close off the grotto."

"It's what a lot of people come for. It's the main attraction, really. Next to the xylophone."

"We can give a reduced ticket. Hope enough people decide to come down even if it's not a full show."

"Oh, we're going to lose a bundle, aren't we?" Jesse says. "Why couldn't this happen in January?"

He picks up her right hand, puts the left on his shoulder. "Sweetheart. What say we do the Dance of Minor Cave Dilemmas." He pulls her into the corny fox trot he uses to sidestep bad moments. He can't stand for her to have any. "Heaven," he sings into her ear, the notes so close they buzz in her ears. "I'm in heaven. And my heart beats so that I can hardly speeeeeak." He twirls himself out and snaps back in, Gingering her Fred. "And I seem to find the happiness I seek. When we're out together dancing cheek to cheek."

They shuffle awhile, which they can do only with a bit of difficulty. In addition to being pregnant, Jesse, at six feet, stands several inches taller than Neal. She stoops a little and stretches her arms and they box-step around the worn floor of the cave.

"We're doing great," he tells her.

"We are, aren't we?" she says, as though his saying it
makes it true.

"Sure we are. You're selling houses like hotcakes. And if
we come up a little short, my family can kick in. They're
doing great with the little Balkan circus. They've even got
winters into the black now, with the clown college. We've
got prosperity floating all around us. We should save our
worries for the hard times. These aren't them. These are the
times we're going to look back on from the hard times as
our golden moments."

While she's dancing, Jesse closes her eyes and looks
through to their future. There's she and Neal and Willie
and the baby and the camcorder Neal hasn't bought but
surely will, so he can over-record Olivia's life. There they all
are, filling the frame. There's no room for anything else.
Not so much as an inch at the margins for an edgy sky-
writer.

"I might stay down here a little while," she says, sitting down on the bench along the wall. "Cool out. You
know."

He nods, and looks at her in a way that makes her see
that he knows. Maybe not that it's Wayne. Maybe not even
that it's someone. But she can tell he feels the displace-
ment of the energy she usually has for him. Maybe he has
been putting it down to the pregnancy, to some hormonal
flux. But what about after the baby is born? She suddenly
feels a flush of sickness, which she hasn't experienced since
the earliest days of her pregnancy. She's enraged at herself.
She doesn't want the tacit knowledge of her faithlessness —
her unspoken confession met by Neal's unspoken forgive-
ness — corroding the connection between them.

*

Once he has left and Jesse is alone, she sits against the wall and tilts her head back so she can look into the blue of the vaulted ceiling. She is feeling her present pressing in on her. She needs to get away. And so she closes her eyes and makes the blue go to aquamarine. This is how it happens. Inside her lids the color gets born again. First in a flat wall, then fragmented, smashed into wavy panes, the way a pool bottom looks when the water is broken by swimmers, shot through with sun. Aquamarine and then the slap of her hand on tile and she's coming up, shooting out of the water for the hundredth, the thousandth, time.

The color is a straight shot back. From here she can clear the frame of blue-green and let in the dead white. The night before their event, down in the showers. The part she dropped from the story as she told it to Alice Avery. She and Marty lying next to each other on those vast, soft piles of towels. The white tile pulling in moonlight through the open windows, a drip in the near distance — rapid, urgent. And farther off, wild dogs howling through a restless night of their own.

"What?" Jesse hears herself whisper. She is seventeen, with all her stores of curiosity intact.

Marty props herself up on an elbow, so tan she looks black against the backlighting of the tile.

"I broke fifty-nine. Fifty-eight-forty."

"You lie."

"I don't," Marty says. "That's the thing. You know I don't."

"How come it's not all over the place, on the gossip lines?"

"It was last night, late. Everyone was gone. Only Ian was with me. He clocked it."

"Ian might have a lousy watch."

"Might. Never can tell," Marty says.

Jesse laughs, both because she's nervous about being down here in the middle of the night, and because here they are, at the Olympics, and Marty's trying to pull the cheapest sort of club pool psych-out.

"Fastest," she whispers now, tapping her own heart. Then, tapping Jesse's, she says, "Second fastest. Everyone else eats our wake."

Jesse stands listening to her pulse pounding in her temples, and to the dogs, for the light years until Marty says, "Seems to call for something, doesn't it?" Even though the words are spoken low, they seem to Jesse — wholly unversed in the mechanics of seduction — to ring off the tiles. Even though it is the lightest imaginable touch, Jesse feels the whorls of Marty's fingerprints burning into the soft skin at her throat.

And that's it. She can't push it any further, although there surely was a further. As hard as she can stare at the insides of her eyelids, she can't bring the colors back.

Neal is easy to wake up, even in the middle of the night, even when he's on his back with his mouth open, looking like a fighter on the canvas, out for the count. She touches him and his eyes pop open.

"The baby!" he says, startled, but alert, ready to go.

"No, it's just me. I'm all riled up."

He rolls over and props himself on an elbow and touches the scar at her jaw. She wonders how he can even find it in just the moonlight.

"It's the air conditioning," he says. "It throws the ions in the atmosphere out of kilter. I read it somewhere. If the heat keeps up, we should really just go down and sleep in the cave."

"No. It's my past."

"Your checkered past?"

"My aquatic past. I took Alice Avery out to the quarry today. She remembers me from back when. Something about that nerves me up. Gets me to thinking old thoughts."

"But all that's over, dead and done, a million miles behind you."

She rolls away from him, looking for comfort in what used to be their old spooning position, only now she's too big for him to get his arm around her. She rolls back in frustration and props herself up on bunched pillows. "I worry I was my best self then, my best version of me. And I can never get back to her."

He sits up, too, and looks down at her. "Sweetheart, I've known you the whole time between then and now. I'm practically an authority on you. Ted Koppel will have me up on the screen when he does a 'Nightline' on you. And I'll tell him that you were great when I met you, a wonderful girl and all, but really just at the start of you. I knew I was taking a big chance."

This is the kind of place where she usually gives him a fake punch in the stomach, but she doesn't have the heart now.

He goes on anyway. "All you really were then was great-looking and incredibly fast in water. All the really good parts have been filled in since then. You just can't see it because you're sitting on the inside. Lucky you've got me with twenty-twenty to set you straight."

Jesse grabs onto his beard and starts to cry softly, silently, just tears sliding out the corners of her eyes. She has never told him about the aquamarine, or even much about Marty. Jesse has been with Neal more than twenty years chesting these trumps. And yet she let almost all of it come tumbling out to Alice Avery today. In the same off-balance way, she has not really ever let herself experience passion with Neal, who has thrown his whole lot in with hers. Has instead squandered it, on two near strangers.

Jesse and Wayne are sitting across from each other in a semicircular black vinyl booth in the cocktail lounge of the Holiday Inn by the interstate. They come here because there's no one else but them and tourists and passing-through salesmen. It's two in the afternoon. She's having a Coke, Wayne's having coffee — he drinks it all day long, mostly from Styrofoam cups with half-moon holes punched in the tops.

He's panicked. She has just told him she can't see him anymore until after the baby is born. She meant to say she can't see him again ever, but she had a last-minute failure of nerve. She is sure that in two or three months he will be onto something else, maybe even another town, and she will be safe. Right now, though, she's not safe at all. She's trying to rescue a flailing man while going under herself.

"You could come with me," he says.

"I'm not going anywhere."

"I could come up with something wonderful," he says. "We could go to Florida. I could skywrite over those long beaches full of college kids. You could teach swimming at a hotel pool. You could teach the sidestroke to old ladies. We could eat fried fish dinners and go to the drive-in for a movie at night." This is a scheme pulled straight out of his desperation, but she knows he'll punch it up into real life around her if she gives him a chance.

"The baby," she says.

"The baby would be our papoose. We'd put her in a backpack and bring her along. Wherever."

But there is no wherever for them. At this moment, Jesse feels a sharp catch beneath her breastbone, the price exacted for creating this thought, the thought of really never seeing him again. She also feels a lilting relief. She is standing in a red velvet and sequin bathing suit, inside the exploding burst of magician's smoke. When it clears, she'll be gone.

• • •

They're having Thanksgiving at Hallie's this year, more or less by default. Jesse, who usually has it at her house, has been too frayed and short on sleep with the baby, who has turned out to be a happy and easygoing, but nocturnal creature. Having the dinner at Frances's was out of the question; she's a notoriously terrible chef. And everyone agreed Alice spends enough time in the kitchen the other days of the year and should be able to just put her feet up for the holiday. She and her lover, Jordan, have been invited on the condition they don't complain about lumps in the gravy.

It turns out to be a particularly fun afternoon. The balance is just right. Frances comes by herself. Darrell is off at one of his daughters' in some extremely backwoods Arkansas hollow, where the traditional holiday main dish — Frances informs them as though Darrell is from another country — is fried wild hare.

"Road kill," Jesse says under her breath to Neal.

Frances is totally taken with Alice, considers her sophisticated for being from Kansas City, and a restaurateur. This fascination takes her attention off Jesse and Hallie, who she doesn't enjoy seeing together. Today though, they can just hang out in the steamy kitchen with Hallie doing the real cooking while Jesse takes the easy jobs — cutting the canned cranberry jelly into slices, folding the Cool Whip into the Waldorf salad — while extending a toe to jostle Olivia, who sits cackling in her bouncer. Neal watches football on TV in the living room with Willie, who enjoys the game for what must be reasons of his own, since he can never find the ball in any given play.

After a while, Willie comes back, wanting the baby, making gimme signs with his outstretched hands. He is quite proprietary about her. Not that he thinks she is his, in the sense of being her father. It's more like he assumes Jesse has brought Olivia into the world for him.

"Okay, okay," Jesse says, and pulls her daughter out of the contentment of her bouncer and hands her up to Willie. He adores the baby, is serious and overly careful with her.

When the turkey is out of the oven and cooled down a bit, Neal comes back into the kitchen to wield his electric carving knife. "A *man's* job," he says in a bogus macho way, waving the buzzing knife over his head.

They all take places on regular chairs and folding ones brought up from the basement, wedged in next to each other in Hallie's small dining room. Frances, who is the only regular churchgoer in the group, says the blessing, thanking God for Olivia (with whom she is still tentative, edging slowly into grandmotherhood) and for "new friends."

After dinner, after the coffee and pies — pumpkin, mince, and chess — have gone around, they all groan and push themselves away from the table and totter off, either to clatter away in the kitchen with dishes and leftovers and vast sheets of foil and plastic containers, or to find soft spots in the living room, where they can collapse and digest.

Jesse takes Olivia upstairs to nurse her, something they both enjoy. Jesse is nuts about this baby. She couldn't have guessed this. She had no idea she had this particular set of feelings inside her. A lot of the time it's as though she is drunk with love. And it's a right love, about something real and permanent. Not some riling thing making all the hairs on her neck stand up and setting everything else on edge.

All that is behind her; she can feel herself sealed away from it. She has put it on the other side of the liquid wall she sees as the border of her life as she's living it. Beyond this, hidden from view, are the rejected choices, like Wayne.

Also the unmade ones. Even though she can't see these clearly, she feels them pulsing out there, all the unmet others, all the untried ways of pushing against the fates. She knows they exist, though, by the shape of their absence, by the shadows she can just barely make out on the other side of the membrane.

When she has put the baby down for a nap, Jesse joins the others in the living room. The TV is on one of the soaps, but not the right one. Everyone's talking, though, nobody's really watching, and so Jesse picks up the remote and clicks it to "M.D./R.N." Rhonda is on the witness stand, lying about where she was on the night of Stephen Poole's death. (The net is closing in on her.) But Jesse is not really listening. She's bothered by the bandage on Rhonda's hand. She has been wearing it since sometime in late summer. Supposedly this was about an accident in her kitchen, something she did to herself on account of being rattled about the murder. Jesse never bought this. Anyone with the presence of mind to shoot a guy, then stuff him into a garment bag and drag him out of her apartment and down the service elevator and dump him into the river with dumbbells tied to his wrists and ankles is not going to accidentally stuff her hand in the food processor along with a bunch of carrots.

They try not to show it — the hand — but this is hard in close-ups, like now, when Rhonda is bursting into tears in the courtroom (a big show for the jury), sobbing violently into her hands, one of them wrapped tightly in gauze. She suspects the hand problem is not Rhonda's, but rather belongs to the actress who plays her. She'd like to know what happened. It bothers her to seem to know whatever there is to know, to operate on all the information that's offered, and still be missing some piece of knowledge, the one that would make everything come clear.

This has been the first blue day to surface from weeks of gray, and the afternoon is in its last spectacular moments as they head home. Jesse is driving, Neal next to her in the front. Willie is catnapping in the back. The baby, in her car seat, is patting the top of his head and making soft noises, a private song.

"Eighty," Neal says. He always keeps a casual eye on the speedometer when Jesse's driving. She lifts her foot off the accelerator, and simultaneously lifts her eyes from the road in front of them. There on the clean slate of sky is a smoky script being scrawled by a plane, just coming off the loop of the final "e" of Jesse. Her heart takes a thrilling deer's leap and she feels her fingernails cut into her palms around the steering wheel.

It's hard to pretend not to notice skywriting, but Neal manages.

Old Souls

JESSE IS STANDING at the cabinet in her carrel in the literature stacks, filing away notes on Flannery O'Connor for a book she's writing about the influence of illness on certain twentieth-century American writers. In this research phase she has become both mesmerized and profoundly depressed. There are times when she wishes she were writing instead on the influence of puppet shows on certain American writers, the influence of clowns tumbling out of small cars. Hurled cream pies.

These back stacks are among the few truly quiet places in Manhattan. They look out onto an ivy-clogged courtyard, a souvenir from another New York. The only sounds are internally generated ones — the occasional rustling of papers being gathered up, the soft thwack of book covers being shut, a constant fluorescent hum. But now there is a sudden rush of air, the sharp clank of a bangle bracelet hitting the shelves, followed by Kit sailing in breathless. Finding Jesse, she stops short, her elbows lofting a little as she slams out of forward, into neutral. She often arrives this way, as though she has been missing for years, shipwrecked and given up for gone, but now — astonishingly — here!

In fact, it has been less than three hours since they last saw each other. Jesse looks down. She doesn't like Kit to see how strongly she is affected by her; it seems a little absurd even to Jesse.

Anyone could walk back here, although it is summer and Friday and late in the afternoon, and so probably no one will. Still, Jesse feels the dead atmosphere of the room begin to crackle a little with risk as Kit presses her back against the jutting handles of the file drawers, tugs her shirt free, and runs her hands up Jesse's back and then around, tracing her breasts.

"I think," Jesse says when her mouth is freed up, "that if I get fired from a tenured position, I'd especially like for it to be on account of the morals clause."

Kit puts her hands behind Jesse and pulls her in.

"Maybe we'd better go home," Jesse says. "Start our vacation."

Kit nods, kind of hearing.

They walk on an angle through the Village. Kit gets stopped by a flurry of teenage girls. Jesse thinks, boy, teenage girls these days sure look like hookers. Then she notices one of them negotiating with a guy in a delivery van and realizes these girls *are* hookers. They are also fans of Kit, and want her autograph.

Kit is an actress of sorts. She plays Rhonda, the vampy intensive care nurse on a terrible hospital soap. Five days a week, she has to Rhonda around in an extra set of eyelashes and outfits that are as provocative as possible within the limitations of their also being white uniforms. Wardrobe has also worked up a sexy nurse's hat for her.

When she first came on the show, Rhonda was almost immediately given a juicy euthanasia subplot. She was accused of pulling the plug on an intensive care patient, an old guy who only days before he died, changed his will to generously include Rhonda. Since this story line was resolved, though (it turned out there had been an inadvertent mix-up in medication charts), for months all the scripts have let Rhonda do is lurk suspiciously around the medicine room, and vamp through her mirrored apartment in slinky hostess gowns and earrings that hit her shoulders, entertaining married doctors. Kit was worried they were going to write her character out entirely, but now she's gotten a break. Rhonda has shot the latest of the married doctors after he laughed at her ultimatum that he leave his wife.

This week, she has been busy scrubbing bloodstains out of her carpet, dragging the body out in the dead of night to the river, where, before pushing it over the bridge railing, she tied dumbbells to its wrists and ankles. Without a corpse, Rhonda's guilt is going to be difficult to prove, and Kit figures she has at least several months more of employment while Rhonda acts coyly innocent in the face of strong suspicion. The show is taped two weeks in advance, so they can write her onto a back burner and she can slip away to Missouri tomorrow for a few days, and go home with Jesse.

While the teen hookers are pulling scraps of paper from their oversized purses, Jesse ducks into a small record shop and buys a tape for the trip. When she comes out, the girls are gone, but have been replaced by a middle-aged woman and her mother, trying to cajole plot revelations out of

Kit — specifically whether Dr. Silva and Louise the hospital administrator are really the leaders of a satanic coven. Wordlessly and rudely — it's the only way — Jesse pulls Kit free and off up Christopher Street.

"Next time anybody asks me for an autograph," Kit says, "I'm going to say, 'Well, where's your autograph hound then? I only sign stuffed hounds and leg casts.' " Kit doesn't — can't, really — take her celebrity seriously; it's only based on a moderate-sized part in a daytime drama, and some commercials for a dandruff shampoo. If she's at all pretentious — and this takes a bit of wine and some prompting — it's about her aspirations, which hover in Meryl Streep range.

"I'm going to cook tonight, something special," she says now.

Jesse draws a fingernail across the inside of her own wrist, miming the opening of a crucial vein.

"Be nice," Kit says.

They kill each other with kindness in the kitchen. Both of them are deadly cooks. Jesse is bonded to her godmother's red plaid cookbook from the fifties. Everything she makes is baked for an hour at 325 and covered with white sauce and sometimes crushed potato chips, or molded in freezer trays and topped with maraschino cherries.

Kit is of an opposite persuasion. "Civilization has advanced beyond the plaid book," she says. She careens into the elaborate and exotic. Cuisines from the fourth world, the deepest folds of the Himalayas. She shops in the darkest of ethnic groceries, rummages through the dusty cans on the back shelves, the inscrutable plastic-shrouded items lurking in the smoky depths of the freezer. She has involved, labored conversations with shop owners, then with their ancient mothers brought out from curtained back rooms. By this time, Kit is taking notes on check deposit slips, buying additional, amazingly authentic condiments.

The end result of these flurries goes like this: Jesse arrives home. The hallway of their building has a malevolent odor. She immediately worries that Mrs. Levine in the garden apartment — the oldest person Jesse has ever seen outside of those yogurt ads — has finally expired, and everyone has been too busy or self-absorbed to notice.

But the peculiar smell only gets stronger as she climbs toward her own apartment. Inside, the odor is almost visible. Several pots burble ominously on the stove.

"What is it?" Jesse will say, skipping past the pleasantries.

"Well . . . you like steak, don't you?" Kit will say in a desperately cheery voice.

"I like steaks when they come from cows," Jesse says. "Cows who, when they were alive, lived in America."

"Well, this is just the Burmese version."

"Kit. If there's lizard in any of those pots . . . "

At this point Kit's eyes begin to water up.

"Oh no," Jesse says, rushing over to hold her. "There really *is* lizard in one of those pots."

"But *only* one."

"Don't cook," Jesse says when they're inside the door. "It's way too hot. We'll go out."

Not right away, though. They fall onto the futon, pulling off some of their clothes, forgetting the rest.

A while later, Jesse asks Kit, "Are you about to come?"

Kit nods.

"Can you not?"

Kit laughs. "Maybe. Just."

Jesse stands and pulls Kit off the futon. "Let's go. We'll be back. Later. Now though, you'll have something to think about during dinner." Jesse holds Kit in a light sexual thrall. Who knows how long it will last. And anyway, Jesse figures all the real power is on Kit's side of the equation.

When they get back, they drag the futon up onto the roof, near the washtubs of potting soil in which Jesse is cultivating an urban garden of hybrid tea roses. The petals, deep red in sunlight, now look black and give off a heavy night musk. Here, Jesse and Kit begin again, then sleep under the stars and above everyone's music. Then wake and watch the moon travel across the deep black sky.

The next morning, Jesse takes the mail key downstairs. It's only eight-thirty, but Carmen stands in her doorway like a lesser goddess of the demimonde, backed by dim lights and a thin haze of blue smoke. Lou Reed is on the stereo. Samuel, her boyfriend, is lounging on the sofa. He owns a few laundromats, which seem to spin and tumble along on their own. Jesse thinks Carmen and Samuel might be the ultimate party animals, that they could write their own weekly column for the *Voice,* just about what happens in their apartment.

Once Jesse went down to borrow a screwdriver, and Carmen and Samuel were starting the day with one of their panatela-size joints and offered Jesse a hit. Why not, she thought, and then lost the whole part of her life that happened between exhaling and finding herself at the checkout counter of the Korean minigrocery down the street, having just bought three Hostess chocolate fried pies.

"You'll be back when?" Carmen says now.

"In a week. We're going to see my mother. In Missouri."

"Ah," says Carmen, closing her eyes and smiling dream-ily. "The Show Me State."

It astonishes Jesse, the things people know.

Later, she's clipping a borrowed fuzz buster onto the visor of the rental car while a couple of teenagers, unasked, squeegee the already-clean windshield.

"No thanks," Jesse says to the palm sliding through the open window in front of her face.

"Man you shoulda said something *before* we did such a nice job for you."

"I'll leave you something in my will. It'll be like that gas station attendant and Howard Hughes."

Coming originally from a small town, Jesse is given to just the sorts of mildly witty comebacks that get people knifed in their hearts every day in this lower end of Manhattan. This time, though, the fates conspire kindly around her. Kit comes down the front steps and gets in the car just as a coplike vehicle rounds the corner (it turns out to be some-thing bogus like environmental patrol), and the squeegee guys sulk over to the curb.

Jesse clicks her tape in as Kit pulls out. It's Springsteen's "Nebraska." "Open All Night" comes up.

> Fried chicken on the front seat
> She's sittin' on my lap.
> Both of us poppin' fingers
> On a Texaco road map.

Kit smiles from deep inside the ethos of "trip." For a couple of weeks now, she has been expressing longing for "the road," and making statements like, "Living in New

York is like living in an extremely interesting shoe box." And now she's R.T.G. — ready to go — in traveling clothes. Hawaiian-print bermudas and a T-shirt that says I EAT MY ROAD KILL. She has her blond hair gelled up and back into some kind of surfer retro. She looks like Jan, or Dean.

"All *right*!" she says, pushing her shades up onto the bridge of her nose, shifting into third with just her fingertips as they ramp onto the interstate, pinky-tapping the turn signal as she glides across three lanes.

"Are you nervous? About bringing me?" she asks Jesse in southern Ohio. They're sitting across from each other in a big booth in a restaurant–truck wash along the highway. The restaurant part is the Home of the Dorisburger. Jesse is stretching her bent arm over her head, trying to pull out the kink inside her right shoulder blade, an old weak spot, a vestigial reminder of some punishment her body absorbed during its training days. She shakes her head in response to Kit's question, lying. She has no idea how she's going to mesh Kit with Missouri. Plus there is so much stuff that now seems necessary to explain.

"Don't go crazy with this," Kit says, seeing that Jesse is fretting. "Everybody always feels like their family scene is too weird to translate for someone in their present. You don't really need to tell me anything. I probably won't even see any of the bad stuff. Everyone'll be nice to me just because I'm with you. And I already think you're the most wonderful person in the world, so you don't have to worry about my opinion of you. It's locked in." She taps her heart with a forefinger.

"Still . . ."

"Okay," Kit says. "Go ahead and wrestle those old alligators of your past. But don't worry about me. They're your alligators, they won't bite me."

Every time Jesse comes back to Missouri, she tries to prepare herself, get the issues lined up, sorted out, internally addressed so she doesn't get ambushed by them when she's there. This, of course, never works. Once home, the same faulty systems kick in — everything out of whack and running full steam at the same time. She is almost immediately sucked into trying to impress her mother, and trying to dismiss her. Feeling far above and beyond New Jerusalem, and at the same time romanticizing it like crazy. Longing to be instantly away, and alternately to stay forever, spend her days with Hallie, move with her and William into a house with a wide porch on Broad Avenue.

"What's chicken-fried steak?" Kit says from behind a giant laminated menu. "Does it have chicken in it, or what?"

"Oh, honey," Jesse says, thinking of the week ahead.

Kit and Jesse have been together half a year. One night Jesse was supposed to have dinner with Leo Swift, who teaches all the Victorian courses in the department, and is far and away her favorite colleague. Leo is how she imagines the Bloomsbury boys were. Maynard Keynes. Saxon Sydney-Turner. He seems to her a true scholar. Always lit from within over a connection discovered, an influence discerned, always bearing down on a monograph deadline, pressing into the night as though the world will awaken the next morning in urgent need of coffee and literary criticism.

They share an office in the department's basement quarters, and often when Jesse arrives in the morning before a class, Leo's presence is still hanging around in the air.

Peppery cologne, dry-cleaned wool, butterscotch. So she knows he's at most an hour or two gone.

One morning into the second month of a terrible broken heart Jesse was languishing with (she hoped in a quiet way no one was noticing), he asked if she would like to come to dinner with him that Friday.

"There's a new restaurant on Thirteenth Street that serves food of the Southwest. Do you think that would be interesting?"

And then on Friday, he asked, by the by, if she'd mind if his niece joined them. Something, nothing really, made Jesse think the niece would be a girl, a teenager. And so she wasn't expecting a woman, wasn't expecting a dyke, and especially wasn't expecting someone so blond and tan and better-looking than regular people to such a degree and in such a put-together way you knew right off that the looking good was part of what she did for a living.

Jesse wanted to resist being influenced by this. She didn't like to think looks played a big part in what attracted her to other women, although when she thought about it, the bookstore owner and the flight attendant and the taxi driver–performance artist and the investment analyst and the house painter, and one of the two radiologists (she met one through the other) on the slightly longer than she would like (now that they comprised her past, her permanent sexual record) list of women she had been involved with were actually quite good-looking. But still, none like this.

"Flake off," Kit said when she sat down, looking seriously into an invisible camera. It was the name of the product, and her tag line on the ads. "I'm supposed to say it in a sexy way. No mean feat." She had just landed a five-commercial deal as spokesperson for a dandruff shampoo. The night turned into a small celebration of this small piece of good fortune, in spite of Jesse being a little pissed at Leo for not giving her fair warning about this matchmaking, and in spite of her being leery of Kit's looks, and the fact that she was an actress, which seemed almost to guarantee self-absorption.

At some point probably too early on, Jesse could feel herself throwing caution out the window and running all her internal red lights. She began letting herself sink into deep focus on Kit, who was just smiling and sitting down and acknowledging Leo's introductions and saying "flake off" — performing perfectly ordinary social mechanics in a perfectly unflashy way. Yet at the same time, occupying the available space with molecules that were traveling faster than normal, achieving higher density. Everyone else's had to shift a little and rearrange themselves to make way. Jesse was made goofy by this, and then somewhere around the second margarita, Kit began to reply in kind, paying an elevated attention to whatever Jesse said, responding to her remarks as though they were particularly droll or perceptive or whatever.

Oh boy, Jesse thought, staring for way too long at the puddle of salsa on her plate. And then felt a flush run through her entire body when their fingertips brushed, not quite accidentally, amid the blue corn tortilla chips.

And then later, when Leo was insisting on picking up the bill and Jesse was thanking him and saying good night, Kit was coincidentally heading just Jesse's way and so why didn't they get a cab together? And then why didn't Jesse come up, Kit had some Kona coffee she'd just bought herself as a treat.

In the time it took the creaking freight elevator to ascend the five floors to Kit's loft, Jesse, traveling on a light gloss of margaritas, figured, What the hell, if there was a seduction going on, why not co-opt it? She pressed a hand against the scarred metal wall next to Kit's head, leaned in, and kissed her.

"This is so — " Kit started to say.

"Oh, come on. Not *so*."

Two weeks later, Kit left a toothbrush of commitment in the glass on Jesse's sink. A month after that, Jesse sublet her small one-bedroom and Kit sold the loft, so they could start fresh in a place that was neither hers nor hers, but theirs. Aided by Jesse's shrewd scouring of ads and following up of leads, and Kit's ridiculously wonderful salary, they got a small but pretty apartment on a relatively quiet block off West Broadway. Of course, this was pure recklessness in Manhattan. The romance could expire, and Jesse could be out on the streets, looking for an apartment half as nice as the one she'd just given up, which had taken her two years to luck into. At first, she was impressed with her own daring. Now she worries it was ridiculous impulse, and that it has added another weight on Kit's side of the delicate balance. Too much when added to her also loving Kit too much. "Too much" being more than she suspects Kit loves her.

In the past (with the exception of the heartbreak she was nursing when she met Kit) Jesse has always been light on her feet through the course of relationships, and at their ends, halfway out the door before the other person could even get up from her chair. With Kit, though, her steps are slowed and softened, as though she's walking through loam. There'll be no running away. She'll stay until Kit ends it, probably even past that for a while of wordless calls to Kit's phone tape, of turning up at restaurants and parties where Kit might be found, while trying not to appear to be looking for her.

Loving Kit strips all the coating off her nerves. It wasn't until after she met her that Jesse took her first Valium, or saw "Painting with Pamela," which is on cable at three-thirty A.M. Now, when she waits for Kit to show up at the apartment, she sits in the window looking down, counting people who come around the corner, stopping at one hundred and going back to one again. Feeling as though she has eaten and is trying to digest something large and made of rubber. It's a lot like the Olympics. It's the first time since those hundred meters in Mexico City that she hasn't felt any buffer between her and the sequence of events she walks through which make up "her life." This is probably good, a step in personal growth. She hates it.

While Kit has settled so easily into the relationship, Jesse can't seem to come down off the romance of it. This is rattling. She sees herself as a grounded person. She really listens to her dental hygienist when she advises flossing every night. She's a hard grader on student papers and tries to be critically rigorous in her own writing. She sees things in terms of moral dilemmas and winds up pressing on with this sort of conversational tack even when people don't want to hear it, when they just want to dance.

In the abstract, she would say love should be an extension of respect, and yet she doesn't think anything as rational as this accounts for what she feels about Kit. She worries Kit could tell her she secretly dumped toxic wastes in rivers at night and Jesse would still love her, that what she really loves is not Kit — not who she is, certainly not how she looks, the aspect of her that initially attracted and frightened Jesse and which now seems so integral she couldn't say if Kit is good-looking or plain, only that she is Kit-looking. Rather what she loves is how Kit makes her feel. Lighter, aerated with something like thrill. And she worries that it's way too late for her to be feeling this. It's goony. It's as though, at thirty-nine, she's on her way to some cosmic prom.

Fifteen hours of interstates, and Jesse, now behind the wheel, turns with a wide sweep of headlights across tall grass, onto 54 heading southwest. For a brief flash of crossroads — Kingdom City — the night is white with the arc lamps of gas stations and minimarts, drawing into their light an edgy population jacked up on Cokes and coffee and maxing the speed limit.

"Look," Kit says, pointing as she emerges from sleep. They're coming up on a trailer park with a lit neon sign. MEADOW ESTATES—CHRISTIAN FOLKS IN MOBILE HOMES.

Jesse just says, "Mmmm."

"Guess it's pretty hard to get fireworks around here," Kit tries again as they pass the twentieth tourist-trap tent-store. "Or walnut bowls."

"Mmmm."

"Ah. We must be getting close. To where the heart is."

"Where I can never go again," Jesse says. But Kit has guessed wrong about what is preoccupying Jesse. She isn't looking ahead to her mother's house, where the kitchen light will have been left on for their middle-of-the-night arrival. She is looking farther along the loop, to when they get back to New York and Kit will leave her.

She's pretty sure about this. For the past month or so,
maybe a little longer, Kit has been seeing someone else on
the sly. Jesse has no proof, just feels it, like a light breeze
coming in from an open window off to the side. She knows,
for instance, that she will not be the recipient of the post-
card of Imogen Cunningham's "Unmade Bed" she found
yesterday in a card shop bag under Kit's keys on the dining
room table. She's not sure who *will* get it. Most likely
Yvonne Scherr, who plays Mandy, the tough-talking paramedic on Kit's show. Jesse can't stand to imagine Yvonne
coming on strong. The girl is wired for vamping, has smol-
dering looks at her command, like Shanghai Lily. She
brings her own web. It's the sort of fooling around Kit
would think is fun for a while. Jesse suspects this trip is Kit's
farewell offering, that the bad news will be delivered when
they get back.

They're on old Highway 4 now. Rabbits and raccoons
skitter off the thin gravel shoulders, unused to being dis-
turbed at this hour. The night offers no relief from the in-
ferno they drove into around midafternoon. It's as though
the heat was merely absorbed by the ground, which is
now releasing it back into the air. Jesse can feel her back
drenched against the velvety upholstery of the car; her foot
is prickly from being pressed so long against the accelerator pedal. The lights bounce off the reflector letters on the
sign:

NEW JERUSALEM—7 MI

EULA GROVE—23 MI

She cruises past the city limits sign.

Kit opens the glove compartment so she can see Jesse's
face by its light. "Is it weird? Being back?"

"Yeah, that. Kind of nice, too. In a weird way."

She points out the feed store and the houses of a half dozen families she knows. Past the courthouse-library. Past LUNCH. Past what used to be the dry goods store but is now a video rental shop. The Set & Style has its sign flickering in the window, pale white connected letters: REALLY GOOD PERMANENT WAVES THAT LAST.

She drives as though the car is a vaporous phantom rather than a large piece of steel. She takes three red lights as though they're yellows before Kit comments. "Hmmm."

Jesse takes a corner with style. "I lived here seventeen years. Unless someone dies or starts having a baby, I can tell you we're not going to see anything moving at this hour but us."

"I can't believe your mother's sleeping through all this," Kit says after they've dropped a suitcase and rattled the handle of the screen door forever, trying to fiddle it open, and then crashed into a wheeled cutting board cart in the middle of the kitchen, which Jesse doesn't remember being there before.

"Oh, I think we've probably woken her by now," Jesse says. "But she won't come down. She'll want to wait until tomorrow. She'll want to be fixed up proper to meet you, someone new."

Her mother's notions of fixing up have little to do with attractiveness, more to do with old, set forms — short perky hairdos, "daytime" fragrances, slips under dresses, nylons even in deepest summer, handkerchiefs (never Kleenexes). At one time emblems of respectability, these are now also symbols of holding one's own, keeping back from the slippery slope, of stains on a hem, dust on a bookshelf, mold on a shower curtain. From there it's straight onto the skids of lipstick applied without a mirror, pajamas worn into the day.

Jesse hasn't been back here for three years. She is coming now for her mother's sixty-fifth birthday, and her retirement after forty-two years of teaching English at the high school. There will be a party tomorrow afternoon in her godmother, Hallie's, backyard. Nearly all the guests will have known each other all their lives.

There's a note stuck to the refrigerator door with a magnet that's also a laminated card of uplifting verse about kitchens and friendship. The note says, "Have a snack. I've left warmups in here."

"What are warmups?" Kit says eagerly.

Jesse sees that she thinks they are something specific, something regional and delicious, like fritters. She hugs Kit, then disappoints her. "It's just what they call leftovers down here."

Kit opens the refrigerator and looks in, then pulls back out with an accounting. "Fried chicken."

"From the Colonel." Jesse knows without looking. "I'll fix you up a plate."

She starts puttering around the kitchen and gets killed with crummy sentimentality going through the drawers and cabinets, coming across all the old stuff. The plate with the picture of Bagnell Dam painted on it. The scoop they won for naming the new ice cream flavor at Gilley's Creamery one summer — Passion for Peach.

"Bring it on up with us," she says as she hands the plate to Kit. "I'm wiped."

They drag their bags up the stairs with soft thumps. At the door to her room, Jesse puts her hand on the knob, then turns and tries to prepare Kit. "It's kind of a shrine. I mean, I put it up, of course. But even now, my mother doesn't take it down. Which is so weird. She always just dismissed my swimming, always made sure to point out to me what a waste of time she thought it was for anyone with brains. She never even came down to Mexico City. So you figure this out. Of course she's very tricky in giving approval and holding it back. She gives just enough so you understand the other ninety-nine percent is being withheld."

"Maybe she was secretly proud and just couldn't show it to you directly," Kit says.

"It's true I gave her an odd sort of status around here. I didn't come up with a husband or grandchildren, but they named the junior high after me."

"I didn't see that."

"I'd die. I took the long way around so you wouldn't. Come on," she says and pushes against the door.

"Oh boy," Kit whispers. "King Tut's tomb."

The room is filled with gold and silver, colored satin — ribbons and medals and trophies, statuettes of girls in modest bathing suits crouched on starting blocks, electroplated into an eternal present tense, poised for the report of a gun that will never go off.

Kit walks around slowly, like a tourist. She homes in fairly fast. It's hung from a couple of carpet tacks pushed into the plaster — a silver medal on a heavy red, white and blue ribbon. Next to it is a yellowed newspaper photo of Jesse on the second highest, the left of three staggered platforms. All three girls on the platforms have damp hair, arms filled with roses, and smiles brought on with the first ebbing of adrenaline. They have just proven, minutes before this picture was taken, that they are the three fastest women in the world at getting through a hundred meters of water.

"How'd you ever come down off this?" Kit says.

"With quite a thud, I'm afraid," Jesse says.

"What's this?" Kit says now. Jesse has her back turned, pulling a sleep shirt from a canvas duffel. Still, she knows exactly what Kit has found — another photo. Everything inside her jams. Kit holds up the picture in its black wood Woolworth frame. It's an odd photo, taken from behind. Jesse and Marty are both wearing sweatpants pulled on over their tank suits. They are standing side by side in an atmosphere of aftermath, their arms draped across each other's shoulders, waiting for some next wonderful thing to happen.

Kit guesses, "You and the girl who beat you. What's her name."

Jesse turns and tries to gather up a few words. Even a few will do. But she can't. She sits on the narrow bed in this obscure defeat. Kit sees there's a problem and takes charge. She comes over and pushes the bag onto the floor and crawls on top of Jesse. She pins Jesse's wrists to the old chenille-covered mattress and lowers herself until her mouth is on Jesse's ear. "I love that you have something this important you can't tell me about."

Much later, Jesse sits on the floor of her mother's bathroom, in the bluish glow of the shell-shaped light fixture over the mirror. She's drawing a weak chill out of the side of the tub with the heat in her cheek. Her eyes are closed, and behind the lids, everything has already gone to aquamarine. She has shot back a few million moments to the one in which she's slapping the tile at the end of her lane, surfacing to see what the fates have written. Pulling off her cap, shaking her head to drain the water from her ears. As though not being able to hear is the problem, when of course it is actually not being able to know. Looking over at Marty, who's also just breaking through, from the white-noise rush of the water into the cacophony at poolside, the hard, dry surface of the rest of the world, where they will be judged. They have already done what they came to do, won the medals they came to take, made the times that will enter the record books. But what times? Which medals?

And then Bud Freeman is hunkering down in front of Jesse, putting up two fingers, his face free of expression from years of practice at bearing news both good and bad. And in this split second of finding out she has lost, Jesse realizes she was utterly convinced she would win, that all along she hadn't really given any weight to the possibility of losing. It won't take a scaling down of expectation to accept this defeat, but rather a substantial reconstruction of her notion of herself. And she must accomplish this in the next few minutes, before she's out of the pool and dried off and sweatsuited and ushered smiling (the smiling is imperative, imperatively expected) up onto the staggered pedestals, positioned slightly lower than Marty. Who, in the next lane, has just received the flip side of Jesse's bad news, who in her pure joy at having taken the gold is reaching across the lane markers toward Jesse, putting a long arm around her shoulders. She can feel the hot flush of Marty's skin under the cold film of water.

"Told you," she shouts, although in the din no one will hear her but Jesse. "We've won. All the fastness, it's ours."

And for a brief moment — the one Jesse needs to carry her away from the pain scissoring into the wall of her heart — she believes this, buys Marty's version and feels herself being pulled into the next lane, then borne aloft, the two of them arcing into the air, then backflipping into the water, somersaulting along the bottom, skimming the aquamarine floor.

From here, the color of the memory bleaches up to white, the dead white one of the night before. Down in the showers on a wide bed of fresh towels they've scattered on the tile floor, then fallen onto. It's late. Everyone else is upstairs, held in restless, pre-race sleep. In their collective unconsciousness, they are all winning their events, all of them. The beds of this dormitory are filled with gold medals, gleaming like coins overflowing treasure chests.

Floors beneath them, Jesse is lying very still under Marty, feeling the full press of her, taking on her imprint, committing her body to memory. The small, hard breasts. The wide span of shoulder, wider even than Jesse's. Today was Shave Day, a ritual among women swimmers — the *psshhh* of foam, glint of blades across this shower room as months' worth of hair was whisked away to eliminate its infinitesimal drag in the water, to make the body the smoothest, most aquadynamic set of planes possible. And now she is feeling these planes, Marty's hot and dry at the same time, against her own.

She looks over Marty's shoulder, down the long length of the two of them, for they are both tall girls with great, long reaches. When they are swimming, their arms seem to catch the water as though it's a field of a million aquamarine dragonflies. Although they are both fair by nature, a blonde and a redhead, they are extremely tan from summer training and in this peculiar moonlight, against the white of the towels and the tile, their limbs are black.

Jesse's specific sensation in this moment is one of thrill ebbing into safety, of having vaulted over a high bar, and fallen onto a feather bed. The small tugs of doubt about Marty — that maybe this friendship did not come up out of pure impulse and mutual desire, but was calculated, planned — these fears slip away now. Jesse, who is seventeen and touching and being touched for the first time, thinks no two people can be this close and have any secrets from each other.

By the time Jesse wakes up, she is alone in the bedroom, the Imogen Cunningham card propped on the pillow of the other, empty, twin bed. "Try to know me," it says. "Don't make me up. K."

There are traces of coffee and conversation in the air. Her mother and Kit are downstairs in the kitchen. From where Jesse lies, it sounds like everything is humming along nicely without her. The rhythms, the lilt and fall, seem pleasant and superficial. Kit is probably being charming, making life in New York sound "My Sister Eileen-ish," life as it hasn't been lived by anyone in Manhattan for forty years. A whirl of working girl wiliness and colorfully eccentric neighbors and rounds of parties featuring fascinating, but alas impossible, men. Jesse's mother has so far shied away from visiting New York, and so these fictions would be easy to perpetrate.

Jesse doesn't, though. She isn't out to her mother in an explicit way. They've never had a "talk." On the other hand, she has never lied outright, or concocted boyfriends. And she told her mother when she moved in with Kit. And now she has brought her lover home.

*

When Jesse gets downstairs, she sees she was wrong. Up close, the rhythms are not good. Now she's sorry she stayed so long in bed, then in the shower.

Her mother is standing at the stove, waiting by a tea kettle rattling its way to the boil. With age, she is becoming a stark figure, the sort of old woman who frightens small children. She is nearly as tall as Jesse, five eleven or so, and has perfect posture, which only adds to the looming effect. She has always considered her height an attribute rather than an oddity, won Tallest Girl ribbon one year at the Mullen County fair, was never bothered by towering over Jesse's father.

She is thinner every time Jesse comes home, now has the rangy look of the farm women she has always felt superior to. At the moment, she looks even more severe for being tense. Her mouth is pulled tight, tucked in at the corners. Something has gone wrong. Jesse tries to smash through whatever it is with a lot of entrance. She gives a hug and gets back an awkward yank around the waist. Her mother has always been uneasy with physical show. If they were alone in this kitchen, Jesse wouldn't even have tried. But in front of Kit, she doesn't want to seem like Camus' stranger.

"Now that's a sophisticated haircut," her mother says, eyeing but not touching the vaguely New Wavey style Jesse has been wearing for a while. The translation is that she finds it ridiculous, arch. "What do you call it?" The unanswerable question is one of her mother's specialties.

"Am I too late for the good stuff?" Jesse says by way of not answering. This question, too, is a charade. There *is* no good stuff. Her mother hates to cook, did as little as possible until she was rescued by the arrival of frozen foods and prepared dinners and carryout. She had the first microwave in New Jerusalem. She drove all the way to a railroad siding sale in Arkansas to pick it up.

Now she opens the freezer and pulls out a stack of frosty boxes.

"I've got blueberry pancakes. Scrambled eggs with sausage." She lowers her glasses off the top of her head and reads from a package. "Western omelette."

"Pancakes sound great," Jesse says. Her mother opens the box, pulls back the shrink wrap, pops in the tray, slaps shut the door of the microwave, and speed-types commands on the panel of buttonless buttons on the front. She wipes her hands on a dish towel, and sighs, "There." Like Julia Child coming off the sixth vigorous kneading of the croissant dough. "Coffee?"

Jesse nods and watches another teaspoon of instant go into another cup set next to the two already waiting for the water to boil. She can tell that Kit is trying hard. She is wearing loose white walking shorts and a pale blue polo shirt. She has her hair blown out in a soft young-wife style. She's trying to be the most muted and acceptable version of herself possible. She doesn't know something has already gone terribly wrong.

Kit goes upstairs to get the present she has brought, which she refers to as "a little bread-and-butter gift." She has now profoundly entered "country." In the time she has been down here, talking with Jesse's mother, she has already picked up a trace Missouri accent. On the stairs coming down, Jesse heard Kit asking her mother about local crafts. The girl has quilts on her mind, and jams from quaint berries, goose and elder. At thirty, Kit still sees experience as something gift-wrapped in small packages, just for her. Sometimes this aspect of her seems irresistibly ingenuous. Other times, Jesse longs for her to be fifty-five and

Piafesque, someone whose high living is past and anecdotal and expresses itself now mostly in regretting *rien*.

Kit is upstairs long enough for Jesse to lay out a few openings, to give her mother a chance to spill what's bothering her.

"It's a longer drive than I remember. Actually, each time it seems to get a little longer."

"You said she was an actress. I thought, Shakespeare. I don't know. Why didn't you say she was that homewrecker on the hospital show?"

"Oh, Ma. You don't watch that stuff?!"

The lines pull again at the corners of her mother's mouth, giving it an artificial set, like that of a ventriloquist's dummy.

This was the same look, given in this same kitchen, which had caused Jesse to abruptly cut short her last visit, which was supposed to be two weeks long, but ended with her leaving on a night bus to St. Louis after just five days. An unscheduled departure in response to the moment when Jesse's mother, after having disparaged all the important aspects and accomplishments of Jesse's life, looked down over the top of her cup of instant coffee and wondered aloud if Jesse wasn't developing thick ankles, taking after the blunt-shaped women on her father's side.

It was immediately following this remark that Jesse went upstairs to her old room and packed as people in B movies do when they're on their way out of a stormy argument or disastrous marriage — stuffing everything into suitcases with no folding, no concern about tossing shoes in on top of white shirts. Sitting on the bulging cases to get their zippers closed, then exiting the house with the detonation of a slammed door.

Jesse came out this time determined not to mention this

last visit. She actually expected that, because of it, her mother would be on her best behavior. It looks like that's not going to be the case.

"We have a committee at church," she says now, assigning to a higher authority responsibility for her not being able to accept Kit. "S.O.S. Save Our Sinners. We write letters to the shows, the networks. We ask them to take off characters like hers and put on families that reflect Christian values."

Jesse tries for a serious nod, but her mother can smell her amusement, and makes a small, angry sound, a tiny click deep in her throat, and turns away to wash out a couple of glasses with a complicated looking soap-dispenser brush.

"She's not the person she plays on the show," Jesse says, because she can't not defend Kit against any attack, even one as nutty as this.

"Well, I'm sure, but she gives people ideas," her mother says, not letting go now that she has purchase. "Sets a bad example. How'd you even meet a show business person like that, anyway?" she asks now, fixing Jesse with a whammy.

"I teach with her uncle," Jesse says, then wonders if this sounds warm and family-oriented, or like Humbert Humbert recalling how he met Lolita. She watches her mother turn back to the sink and sweep into the soapy water a spatula and spoon rest that says "Spoon" on it.

"Look . . . " Jesse starts, feeling a flash of being up to this. By directly coming out to her mother, she can at least go on the offensive in this conversation, rattle her mother's cage by speaking the unspeakable, break the regional code of polite conversation: that when something is unpleasant or difficult to talk about, it is simply placed on a lower shelf of fact by not mentioning it.

. . . .

"You don't have to tell me," her mother says. "It's on all the shows. Donahue. Oprah." And that's that. Her mother reaches over and tugs the quilted cozy over the toaster and shuts down the subject.

"There's something important I need to discuss with you," she says, further dismissing Jesse's sexuality as too trivial to bother with even while it is too unseemly to mention. A neat trick. She slaps the pump on a bottle of lotion. Too much shoots out and she comes over and strokes the excess onto Jesse's hands. "Darrell and I want to take a long trip this fall," she says. "See the West, in his van."

"What's the S.O.S. going to say about that?" Jesse can't resist.

"I don't care how old you are, I won't tolerate a smart mouth."

Jesse waits.

"We're fixing to get married. Around Labor Day."

Jesse doesn't say anything for a beat too long.

"I know he's not your father. I'm just asking you to respect my happiness."

Jesse thinks for a second. "What are you supposed to say to the bride? I've forgotten. Not congratulations."

"Best wishes."

"Well, you've got mine," Jesse says.

The microwave pings. Jesse goes over, takes out the breakfast. She inhales the steam, which smells like absolutely nothing, then looks up and asks her mother, "What about Willie?"

Her mother sits down across from Jesse, the way the women characters do on Kit's show when they are earnest and anxious. "I was hoping you could take him on for a while. The home's all right so long as he can come here on weekends. They take care of the basics there, but ... I mean, they miss a lot of what's really important. Nobody smiles when he comes into the room. You know. I wouldn't want to leave him there for months on end. He wouldn't starve, but he'd surely wither a bit." She stops, then adds, "I just want you to think about this."

Jesse nods, dragging the side of her thumb across her lower lip, thinking. She is pretty sure right off that she'll do it, even though it will turn her life upside down and shake the change out of its pockets. Kit is thudding down the stairs. Jesse lowers her voice. "Let me talk to her when I can find a right time, will you? I mean, don't mention it just now."

Her mother tightens up again and says, "Whatever."

Kit's present is a sampler of fancy teas. Lapsong soochong, gunpowder, China green. Jesse's mother eyes the brightly colored tins as if they were ticking. "Why, how interesting. I'll have to give a tea party."

Jesse's heart cramps for Kit, her face lit up with what she thinks is success.

Jesse's mother pats the tea tins and looks up at the wall clock. "You girls better run on over and fetch William. I've got some party clothes here for him. When he comes out of there, it looks like he got dressed at a rummage sale."

"Does he know I'm coming?" Jesse says.

"Yes, but I only told him yesterday. Otherwise he builds up to too much of a pitch."

On the drive out, she tries to imagine Kit going along with the plan for William, but can't. Kit came down from upstate New York — Syracuse — because she thought Manhattan would be "hot." Hot is not living with your lover and her retarded brother, probably way out in Brooklyn to afford enough space for three. No, Kit will go with Yvonne Scherr, who inherited a place in the Dakota from her parents, Broadway costume designers. She has parties where everyone tries on her large collection of hats. Kit will definitely go with the hats.

Dismissing her as callow is one of Jesse's hedges against the moment when Kit will leave her. Another is trying to think back on things Kit has said that weren't really all that interesting, or funny. She's trying to put as much cushion as possible between her and the falling stone slab.

Of course, Jesse also realizes that she may be turning up the volume and color simply to make things more interesting. A long-standing tic.

Everyone of course refers to Walnut Farm, where William lives, as the nut farm. Local boys rush up the drive on their bikes, hurl a few insults like rolled newspapers, then peel back out, fishtailing through the gravel as they go. William and his friends, the younger crew at the home, don't seem to take these too much to heart.

They wave back at the boys — variously waving to them and waving them away — then take their insults and turn them on each other in what seems to Jesse a pretty sophisticated defusing mechanism. They call each other "retard" and "dope" and mock each other's idiosyncrasies, as they see them. This is selective appraisal, though, what they consider goofy. For instance, while they seem to find making faces — crossing eyes, waggling tongues, wiggling ears — extremely witty, they consider pratfalls childish. They play to each other a lot and don't let themselves be intruded on too much by an outer world that is always out of synch with them.

The home stands behind an enormous sloping lawn. It is an old farmhouse and a large barn. It's a working farm. Under supervision, the men and women who live here raise vegetables and a small summer cash crop of corn. They keep a dozen milk cows and a coopful of chickens. William likes it here pretty well, he has friends. But he is also always eager by Friday afternoon to come home for two days of a more concentrated sort of attention, a more direct kind.

Everyone is out on the lawn, playing a loose, heat-induced, dreamy variant of baseball. Jesse and Kit get out of the car and sit on the hood to watch. It's as though someone here heard a game or two on the radio, and they're working off that. There are way too many fielders, maybe ten, William among them. And two batters, standing a ways apart. The trick seems to be who'll get pitched to.

"Well," Kit says. "Why not?"

Jesse is smiling with having been discovered. William is loping across the lawn, through the middle of the game. The other players aren't too bothered by this, no more than they are by the sprinkler fanning away in the middle of the field.

She watches William coming toward her and floods with feeling. She can never see him plain and simple, for what he is. He always comes wrapped in their shared past. Jesse's growing up was, unavoidably, a lot about Willie. Because of him, modifications had to be made constantly, the center moved from where it ordinarily would have been, over onto him. Money had to be siphoned off for schools, special programs. Attention had to be paid by all of them in huge amounts to carry him over his frustration at not being understood, not understanding.

And Jesse — by virtue of being normal, regular — was discounted for being so privileged, expected to excel because how dare she not, given such an advantage. She was also expected not to disappear exactly, more to recede into a neutral state of transparency, to not quite fully exist. And so although Jesse loves her brother so much she can feel the muscle of her heart spasm slightly in moments like this, on first seeing him after an absence, she also resents him for having taken up all the available childhood in their house.

He looks less like himself than the last time Jesse saw him, more like a generic retarded person. One of the drawbacks of institutional living, she guesses. He is heavier and walks like his friends, flatfooted, fiddling his fingers in front of him as he goes. It's the walk of a thirty-six-year-old man who has never worn a suit or driven a car or negotiated a deal.

"Boyohboyohboy," he's saying as he approaches. He picks up speed, starts running full-tilt toward Jesse. Then stops short by a few feet and stands there twitching with shyness, running his thumbs back and forth under the waistband of his brown pants.

"Well, excuse me, but have you seen my brother, Willie?" Jesse says.

This sends his gaze rushing with shyness to the ground.

"The last time I saw him, he was wearing blue pants. He did look a bit like you though, I must say."

"Me."

"But no," Jesse says, putting a Jack Benny hand to her cheek and looking him over. "He had long hair."

William runs a hand over his hair, which is cut in a sculptured way Jesse hasn't seen before.

She pats his small belly. "And my brother didn't have this."

He giggles and she gives up the game, letting herself get crushed in a hug. "Oh, Cowboy." Then she pulls back a little to make introductions. "This is Kit."

William nods with sureness and says, "From Ferris."

Ferris is the grade school Jesse went to. It's still there, a block from her mother's house, a fortress of sooty brick and small windows designed to intimidate children. William didn't go there. By that time, they already knew he wouldn't be going to regular school. He would walk Jesse to the corner in the mornings, and be waiting there for her when she got out in the afternoons. The duty girl on that corner was Kitty Hanes. William remembers the most amazing bits of nothing from a million years back, and then goes out forgetting he has put on socks but not shoes.

"No," she tells him. "A new Kit."

But he has become distracted by the baseball game. Everyone is in an uproar. Three or four people are running the bases clockwise. Everyone is clamoring for order, but of many different sorts.

When they finally get him into the car, Kit climbs in back, deferring to William, who then gets in back with her anyway. Jesse chauffeurs them back to her mother's and listens over her shoulder.

"I know a lot about you," Kit says. "Jesse talks about you all the time."

"How?"

"Oh, Willie this and Willie that."

"Willie what?"

"Willie's the best."

In the rearview, Jesse sees his eyes flutter lightly shut, which is what they do when he's blissed out. She wants to stop the car and get out and lift Kit over her head. Buy her all the flowers in some shop. Make her a little cheese soufflé.

When they pull up in front of the house, there's a customized van in the drive. It's iridescent blue with Plexiglas bubble portholes in the side, surrounded by a lush painted landscape featuring pine trees and a running brook and deer, a few rabbits down by the gas tank. On the back, across the door inside quote marks is scripted, *My Way*.

"Darrell," William says.

"Oh my," Kit says, and reaches over the seat back to tousle Jesse's hair.

Jesse hasn't met Darrell. When her mother began mentioning him in letters, Jesse imagined a fat man with small shoulders, bad at golf, full of talk about his grandchildren. Of course, nothing she could have imagined in any direction would have fully prepared her for Darrell. He is such a surprising candidate for her mother's affections that Jesse has had to rethink her notions of who her mother really is.

When the pictures came, Jesse saw he was younger than her mother by about ten years. In style and build and general demeanor, Darrell resembles a white Chuck Berry. Jesse's mother met him through her church social group. Darrell plays pedal steel in a country-rock band that played at one of their dances. Weekends, his group appears at the Blue Light, a notorious roadhouse out by Bedelia. The place is strung with fat blue Christmas lights around the windows, boarded up to keep down the breakage on weekends. A lot of the patrons bring guns with them, to settle questions of etiquette.

"I think Darrell is my mother's equivalent of rough trade," Jesse tells Kit as they get out of the car.

"How does he fit in with her church crowd?"

"She's saving him. They love a lost sheep. She's got him going to Sunday services with her. He's in the choir. I've no idea what her poker-straight friends think of him. It's kind of cute in a way, if anything about my mother can be cute. It's like her little rebellion."

Darrell is fixing something under the sink when they come in — his bony, blue-jeaned hips and legs and silver-toed, snakeskin boots sticking out from the black cave of open cabinet. Jesse's mother is coming up the steps from the basement with warm khakis and a striped polo shirt, fresh from the Ironrite.

"I just pressed these up for you," she tells William. "Let's go upstairs and put them on. There's going to be a party."

"Party down!" William says in an amazingly black voice, snapping his fingers in a jivey way.

" 'Soul Train,' " Jesse's mother says by way of explaining William and then, by way of explaining Darrell, "He's putting in a new catch pipe for me. The old one's rusted clear through."

Work grunts come from the black hole, and then Darrell emerges with a wrench and a battered hunk of pipe. He unfolds himself like a card table into a stooped position and massages the small of his back with the wrench. He's wearing a thin, white, sweated-through sleeveless undershirt, which reveals a tattoo on his upper arm, a rubber stamp picture of a woman in bell-bottom slacks, her hair piled on top of her head. "Cora," according to her caption. Jesse smiles and tries hard not to imagine her mother in bed with Darrell, but she's like a person in the psychology experiment asked not to think of a white bear. She tries to keep at least a sheet over her mother and Darrell, and Cora.

"Ladies," he says. The way he pronounces it, the word ends in *eeeez*. He bows a little, as though asking them to dance. "Jesse, I haven't had the pleasure, and this must be the ac-tress." Darrell's approach is what goes for pure charm and sophistication at the Blue Light, and would probably get him arrested in New York. Jesse can see, though, that underneath this smooth talking, he's a little shy in the presence of celebrity. He pats down the back of his hair with a catlike motion.

"My daughters watch your show. Glued to the set when I get up." This says something about Darrell's schedule; the show is on at three in the afternoon. "They all want to be nurses, like you."

"I guess I didn't know you had kids," Jesse says.

"A few. Here and there," Darrell says, flipping his fingers in the air. "And a few more that thinks they got claims. Nothing that'd hold up in court, though."

Jesse can tell Kit loves this. Of course, it's not *her* mother.

They all ride over to Hallie's in the van. Darrell drives and Jesse's mother sits next to him in a matching velour bucket seat. They hold hands on the shift knob. William tries out one of the bunks along the side in the back while Jesse and Kit face each other in little swivel chairs across the poker table in the center.

"Have a Coke, go ahead, or a Seven-Up," Darrell offers over his shoulder, but no one makes a move. He taps a cassette into the dashboard tape deck and suddenly the van is wall-to-wall with Merle Haggard rolling out "Looking for a Place to Fall Apart."

Kit lowers her eyelids and says in a low voice to Jesse, "Come here often?"

*

By the time the party gets going, it's the hottest part of the afternoon on the hottest day of this very hot — even for Missouri — summer. There are box fans pulled out on extension cords, blocks of ice set in front of them. They don't even make a dent in the heat, or in the deadness of the air.

There are maybe fifty people in Hallie's backyard, and following the custom in these parts, enough food for twice that many. The long row of end-to-end tables are jammed with bowls of salads — three-bean and slaw and sour cream–cucumber. German potato salad. A plate filled with squares of frozen pineapple-cherry salad, already in serious meltdown. Casseroles on trivets — lima bean and tomato, scalloped potatoes and twice-baked potatoes and potatoes Anna. A platter of pea puffs. Three kinds of fried chicken. A large cutting board stacked with barbecued ribs. Desserts alone take up a third of the space. Rhubarb and blueberry and apple pies. Raspberry cobbler. A freezer tub of peach ice cream set in a washtub of shaved ice. A bread roll. Two chocolate cakes. One is plain, the other is frosted with "Happy 65 Frances!" across the top. To Jesse's knowledge, no one has ever called her mother Fran.

Jesse looks around for Hallie, but can't find her, then gets pressed into standing by Darrell and her mother at the head of the buffet so they can greet everyone. Some of the guests are relatives — Jesse's mother's brothers and her father's twin sisters and their children and grandchildren. Some are neighbors, others are teachers from the high school, still others are her mother's students from classes gone by. Jesse wells up with love or something for all of them, wilting a little in their best clothes. They are presents in themselves, as much as the wrapped boxes they bring into the yard along with their covered dishes.

It's hard to imagine this party occurring in New York. Jesse, having slipped out through the gate in the heavy fence surrounding this place, has shut herself away from this experience. In New York, a bunch of friends might get together and celebrate something one of them has done, but this party today is celebrating someone simply for having stayed and endured somewhere long enough to accrue affection slowly, like passbook interest. Even though she has flunked probably a third of the guests in this backyard today for not being able to write a topic sentence.

"Everybody loves your mama," Darrell informs Jesse, and she immediately wonders if this is meant as chastisement, if her mother has talked with him about the strain in their relations. But when he punctuates the statement by pulling Frances under the folded wing of his arm and kissing her at the temple, where her hair has thinned out over the years, Jesse sees the remark is pure pride, in her mother, and in himself for his consumer savvy at having picked such a plum.

Jesse just nods and smiles. She doesn't know quite how to talk with Darrell yet. The two of them haven't yet found the grooves they'll fit in, the small set of running jokes and nonsensitive issues for teasing, which she can already see will come to them with time.

"I've never forgotten *Evangeline*," Bob Weeks is now telling Jesse's mother as he stands, shy as a freshman, shifting from foot to foot in front of her although he's in his mid-forties now and owns the Buick dealership. ("Save a Week's Pay at Weeks'.")

Jesse's mother nods and smiles in confusion until she realizes he's not talking about a classmate, but about the poem.

"When you made us start reading it, I thought I'd never be able to slog through," Bob goes on. "But to this day it's the only poem I can remember one darn line out of."

This seems to Jesse a left-handed and puny offering, but her mother looks to be genuinely flattered and happy.

"You had the best penmanship of any boy I ever taught," she says to Bob Weeks, and instead of looking embarrassed, he beams.

As she and her mother watch the plaid back of Bob Weeks's sport shirt disappear into the crowd, Jesse says, "They really ought to put out a *Greatest Hits of Poetry*. Like those records of just the highlights of classical music. This would have only the lines everyone remembers. You know. 'But only God can make a tree.'"

She meant this to spark camaraderie between them. But she sees just too late that she has diminished Bob Weeks's tribute and one-upped her mother, who, while she pretends to be delighted Jesse has followed in her footsteps, teaching English, actually hates it. For her part, Jesse goes along with the expressed notion that she has followed in her mother's footsteps, when of course they both know she has passed her mother by.

A light plane sputters overhead and a Chicken Little chain reaction starts with one and then another and then everybody looking up into the cloudless sky, across which is sailing a banner reading 65 YEARS YOUNG — GO FOR IT FRANCES!

Jesse's mother throws her head back and laughs in a full-throated way Jesse has seldom heard. "It's our UPS man, Wayne," she tells Jesse. "He's a true live wire." She pauses a moment, then squeezing his arm, earnestly asks Darrell, "Go for what, do you think?"

Mavis and Marlene, Jesse's twin aunts, flutter up. They

are dressed in matching outfits, something Jesse suspects they'd like to do all the time, but hold down to "occasions." Today's outfits are checked sundresses with white sandals. They are trendsetters around here. Marlene's husband refers to them as "The Mod Squad."

"So you're still working at that college?" Mavis says now. Jesse nods.

"Any handsome professors?" says Marlene, who has studied Joan Rivers and Barbara Walters and knows to go for the kill fast.

"The handsome ones are all married," Jesse says, faster still. The twins, though, are onto her. She can tell. Between them, they have five regular children who are making the appointed rounds of life, getting married and having kids of their own and staying in the area and holding down decent jobs, getting promoted and advancing themselves with night classes at the J.C.

In addition to these, though, Mavis has a daughter, Rosemary, who dated hoody guys all along and eventually married a long-haul trucker who periodically lands her in the hospital with black eyes and hairline fractures. Sometimes in the middle of the fights Rosemary calls her mother for moral support. The last time she did this, Mavis hung up and called the police. By the time they arrived, Rosemary and her husband had patched things up and were in bed toasting each other with lambrusco, and Rosemary hasn't spoken to her mother since. Lloyd, the husband, says Mavis is an "agitating influence." Right now, Rosemary and Lloyd are at the far end of one of the long, paper-covered tables, eating ham and corn and drinking lemonade and laughing with old friends and looking like a Country Time commercial.

It is because of Rosemary's failure that Mavis and Marlene are treading carefully around Jesse. Everybody is holding cards they don't want to be forced to play. The twins will speculate later about who Jesse is going to bed with. Kit is extremely girled up for the party, though, throwing them a curve.

Jesse sees her over by the giant Weber packed with foil-wrapped ears of corn. She's surrounded by a small group and appears to be the center of it. At first, Jesse is touched by these small-towners, doing what doesn't come naturally, opening themselves to a stranger. And then she sees Kit sign two autographs and understands that this is about Rhonda. Apparently not everyone in town belongs to Save Our Sinners.

"Why, Jesse Austin, can it really be you!?" shrieks a woman in a dress with a lattice print to it, like the top of a pie. Her hair is shoulder length, curled under in a style Jesse remembers envying on the straight-haired models on the magazine covers of her teen years. The most remarkable thing about this woman, who now has Jesse in a crushing embrace, is that Jesse has no idea at all who she might be.

"It's wonderful seeing you again," Jesse says, leaning back from the hug, trying to see behind this person in the here and now, to who she might have been.

"I wouldn't miss your mother's retirement for anything," the woman says in a vaguely familiar voice. "I still have nightmares sometimes. She's making me diagram some hideous sentence on the blackboard. Something with a jumble of prepositional phrases and subordinate clauses. She's standing right behind me with that long pointer — ready to leap out at my first dangling modifier or split infinitive. I think the whole English language will probably breathe a little easier with your mother out of it."

In the middle of looking at and listening to her, Jesse puts together enough clues to figure out who this plump person wearing pink-framed sunglasses with downswept temples and smelling of brisk cologne is.

"Laurel Staats," Jesse says. Skinny Laurel from grade school with her brown rice lunches, from before that even. Jesse can suddenly remember clear as can be Laurel coming by with a giant box of Crayolas, the one with the sharpener built into the back, the two of them drawing and coloring in pictures of everyone in each of their families.

"Owen now," Laurel says. "I got married."

"Yes. Hallie told me. But aren't you supposed to be living in Timbuktu?"

"Abu Dhabi," Laurel corrects. "But now Claude's got this territory around here, and so I'm back home, for a while at least."

Jesse can gather up enough of the old Laurel, the one she lost track of after high school, to see that she is nerved up in this reunion, cheerier than she really is, rushing to fill in conversational gaps before they have a chance to happen.

"But you're the sophisticated one," Laurel says, framing the nervousness in words. "Living in New York. A college professor. And friends with TV celebrities." She nods across the yard toward Kit, who is talking with a continuous trickle of fans. "All I've been doing is being a housewife in a bunch of American neighborhoods in other countries. It's not exactly the same as being global."

Laurel has put on weight. Her sundress is modest, but has a white elastic belt that accentuates her lalapalooza figure. She looks like Sophia Loren or Gina Lollobrigida in some romantic comedy of the early sixties. It's not how Jesse would have expected Laurel to turn out. She was such a bag of bones. In junior high she had to wear both thick glasses *and* braces, and walked the halls of Kirby (the school since renamed for Jesse) stooped under this double burden. By high school the braces were off and she'd gone to contacts that made her blink as though she had a tic. Now it seems all that, and all the drab cardigan sweaters and bag lunches and babysitting for five younger siblings, was just a chrysalis Laurel has broken out of, moving into this resplendent butterflyhood of middle-class, middle-aged femininity.

"Boy, you sure look different," Laurel says, but something in the way she says it makes Jesse think it's not entirely a compliment. "You know. It's not just the hair, but something through and through."

Jesse laughs in lieu of being able to think of anything to say to this. It's true in a way, and she assumes the questions Laurel is holding under this statement are ones she can't really get into in this heat and this crowd and this occasion, and while holding a pea puff she has just taken off a passing tray. When Jesse has been silent too long, Laurel puts a hand on her forearm. "Now, I didn't mean anything by that."

And then, before Jesse can reply, William is suddenly behind her, his stomach pressing lightly against the small of her back, saying, "Come see." He has no notion at all of polite distance, of allowing people their space. The closer the better. She turns and brings him around.

"You remember Laurel," she says, and he shakes Laurel's hand, but doesn't give any indication he knows who she is.

"Come see," he says again, and tugs a little at the back of her shirt.

"I'd better . . ." Jesse says to Laurel, who tries, "Say, why don't you come by while you're here? Meet Claude and the kids. Maybe we could play some cards, have a few beers."

"Ah . . . well, I'm only here two more days," Jesse says, and then realizes she is confirming Laurel's worst fears — that Jesse is someone who has gotten loose of this place and now thinks she's above it. Laurel thinks she's being snubbed. Which is not at all what Jesse wants. So, to stop this confusion in its tracks, she adds, "But, of course. It'd be great. What about if I give you a call tomorrow? When all this" — she waves a hand to indicate the party — "is over."

What William wants to show her is around the side of the house. Hallie's English bulldog, Sweetie, has just had a litter of puppies. Willie has found them, squiggling around Sweetie in a dresser drawer Hallie has set just inside the door to the cellar, where it is tolerably cool.

"Boy," Jesse says, and drops to her knees next to William. "They're so cute. They look like tiny old guys. So wrinkled and grumpy."

"Beany," William says, pointing to a white one that's sleeping with great sighs.

"He's the cutest, all right," Jesse says. "You want him?"

William doesn't answer, which doesn't mean anything.

"You want to come live with me for a while? In New York?"

"Today?"

"No. At the end of the summer. I've got to get just the right place for us. Paint your room blue. I'll have to see if I can find a place that'll take both dogs and brothers."

William has picked the puppy, which seems boneless,

out of the drawer and put him on his lap. This doesn't make the smallest dent in the dog's sleep. He now lies draped over William's leg, drooling a small spot on the chino cloth. In a fast click of a shutter, Jesse imagines the worst. The dog will have some ruinously expensive ailment — hip dysplasia or skin allergies — and the day program she'll be able to find for William will either leave him to vegetate, or put him to work in some sweatshoppy situation, shrinkwrapping cheap toys. And the apartment will be half a block from the roller coaster at Coney Island, above a cotton candy factory. And of course, Kit will have left long before they even get there. But then, in a sudden rush of hopefulness, in this tiny moment sitting here in the clipped grass of Hallie's backyard, with the party a jolly backdrop and tonight's moon visible in the midday sky, bringing William out, even bringing the dog out, all seems possible, just within her reach.

"What a couple of soft touches," someone says from above. Jesse turns and blinks into the sun. It's Hallie. Jesse stands and hugs her and they rock from side to side, absorbing each other.

"My dear, you've gone and gotten so skinny!" Hallie says. As she pulls back to inspect, Jesse can feel her adding up the black linen pants, white T-shirt, the hair, which is still red, but not Jesse's own red, more the magenta of doll's hair, and the little tortoiseshell Lana Turner sunglasses that don't look like anything anybody else in this backyard is wearing. "I don't know," Hallie says, as though she's being pressured to make a judgment call.

"I'm *fine*," Jesse says.

But Hallie's not conceding the point just yet. "The thing is, sometimes it's hard for a person to know for sure that they're fine," she says. "Sometimes they need a second opinion."

Backing off a bit, Jesse realizes — a realization she has had to repeat each of the few times she has seen her in recent years — that Hallie is not an enormous woman, only a matronly, buxom one. When Jesse was growing up, Hallie in her bulkiness seemed colossal, like a tree, someone to lean into. As far as leaning was permitted — by Jesse's mother, and by the tacit conventions in a small town in the late 1950s, which bound families together and held friends at arm's length, which left doors unlocked but implicitly unopenable.

It has been an odd shuffle — Jesse coming to her mother, who has never accepted her, and being denied to Hallie, who has loved her so fiercely from the start that, as she once confided, she has always had to hold herself back lest she overwhelm Jesse, and appear peculiar to everyone else.

Sometimes Jesse can almost persuade herself that all of this has been for the best, that given free reign, Hallie would have spoiled her rotten, turned her into someone pouty, lacking in wherewithal, whining over failed career schemes, purple marks on her wrist from where the latest lover grabbed her too hard. Someone like her cousin Rosemary. Maybe her mother's rejection was also the cement in the foundation of her character. Maybe.

Although not so dramatically as Jesse, Hallie has also changed with the times. Her hair, which for years was salt and pepper, teased and sprayed into something firmly puffed, now is soft and short and permed, and dyed a minky brown. Her glasses are no longer cat's eyes, but aviators with a tint to the lenses. For this party, she's wearing pale yellow pants and a short-sleeved floral blouse revealing her oddly muscled arms, knotty from years of working over people's scalps.

"So Mama's getting married," Jesse says.

"Well, I imagine that seems funny to you," Hallie says. "Her being so smitten and all. And he's not who you'd expect, it's true. But it's turned her so wonderfully girlish. Dr. Thomas says her arthritis has gone into remission, and you can't tell me there's no connection."

Jesse looks over to where her mother is standing with Darrell. They are talking with Evelyn Pond, the new young principal over at the high school. Darrell, she can tell even from this distance, is being witty. He's holding his cigarette between thumb and middle finger, delicately punctuating his story as he goes.

"No," Jesse says dubiously, "I can see it's a good thing."

"I'm trusting you're going to be nice about this." Hallie says, theatrically arching an eyebrow.

"Come *on*. I'm already working on the song about them I'm going to sing at their wedding." She pretends to be counting a meter in her head, then stops to ask Hallie, "Can you think of anything that rhymes with Rec Vee?"

A heavyset but light-on-her-feet woman bustles up, caftaned and cologned in some scent much muskier than what most of the women here today have on, and bearing — like almost everyone else who has arrived this afternoon — a foil-covered pan of something. She taps the foil with a fingertip and says to Hallie, "Your favorite. Porcini prosciutto risotto."

"Alice here," Hallie says to Jesse, "is changing our taste buds. My goddaughter, Jesse Austin," she adds, completing the introduction.

"Ah. I'm catering your mother's wedding," this Alice says, making Jesse feel excluded, shut out of an occasion that is clearly already well into the planning stage, while she is only up to making fun of it.

William now has all the puppies out of the box and is trying to line them up on the lawn. Sweetie is waking up, cross at finding her babies gone. Hallie hunkers down and tucks the pups back around their mother. She stands up, massaging the small of her back.

"Mama wants me to ake-tay Illiam-way," Jesse tells her.

Hallie nods. "Give you some family. I worry and wonder about you. New York City. Such hard ground to try to take root in."

"I'm not alone," Jesse says, and doesn't feel any danger descending on the conversation. Hallie has always known. She has always been able to read Jesse without anything having to be said to clutter up things between them. Jesse thinks that if love were measurable by an equation that factored in both time and heart space occupied, she has probably loved Hallie Butts more than she'll ever be able to catch up and love anyone else.

They had their astrological charts done once by a man in Hot Springs, Cecil Luster, who said they were both old souls, that they had already lived many lives, the first in ancient Rome. Now they have few left ahead of them. He didn't often see souls as old as theirs. It was some kind of rarity, and accounted, he said, for their friendship. It was a shared wisdom in part, he'd said. And a shared weight of knowing.

"Come see the bath," Hallie says now. In spite of living in a house in which nearly every piece of furniture, including the massage recliner, is from the Sears Early American collection, Hallie has used part of her Harper Method Thrift Plan savings to put in a Roman bath.

She takes Jesse in by the hand, through the kitchen,

where a cake, an Apricot Cloud, Jesse's childhood favorite, sits on the kitchen counter.

"I didn't want the Huns to get to it before you arrived," Hallie says, gesturing out the open window toward her yardful of guests. When they get to the bathroom, she flips on the light switch with a flourish and says, "Well, *veni, vidi, vici.*"

Jesse stands in the doorway in amazement, staring at a huge, round sunken tub, the steps up to it flanked with handled urns. Two alabaster nudes (one male, one female, no fig leaves) in the corners, tiles picturing women carrying baskets, oxen pulling carts.

"It's pretty amazing, but I like it," Jesse tells Hallie, and she's not quite lying. And she promises herself she won't sacrifice Hallie by sending this up to friends back in New York.

When Jesse comes out of the house, she sees that some dancing has started up, on the driveway apron. Somebody has propped a boom box on a folding chair and Whitney Houston has joined the party. Although it's the kids who have brought the music, it's mostly their parents who are uncool enough to dance on a driveway to a radio in the middle of the afternoon. In spite of the heat, Darrell and Jesse's mother even get out and do something restrained and vaguely like jitterbugging.

Jesse watches for a little while, then suddenly pulls away, whiplashed by a sixth-sense radar. Willie loves to dance, thinks he is a great dancer. Why isn't he out here? She turns sharply. Back by the wooden fence at the edge of Hallie's lot, three high school boys — two of them Mavis's grandsons, the Cooney boys, the third she doesn't recognize —

are encouraging William to blow out the fuse on the cherry bomb they've lit in his hand.

Jesse has forgotten the pure dumb meanness that grows up around here as a glandular part of adolescence, in minds running on high idle. In a crushing second she remembers all the cats flambeaux and squooshed things in play lots, and Lewis Frey at the party where he took a gulp of the Clorox-on-the-rocks someone slipped him.

She starts to move, but everything, herself included, has downshifted into slo-mo. She shouts but can't tell whether she's making anything come out. She is in the middle of some wild, flailing leap through the crowd when she sees Kit come off her peripheral vision and get there and grab the cracker.

And then there is only the terrible sound.

And then they're in the back of Darrell's van, doing it His Way to the hospital rather than taking the time to wait for the ambulance. Jesse is holding Kit's right hand inside an oven mitt stuffed with crushed ice — Hallie's idea. Kit is on the bottom bunk, breathing with long, grinding exhales. Her eyes are glossy with pain backed by panic.

"Two minutes to the hospital," Jesse says, looking out one of the portholes. She looks down at Kit, still astonished. "They're going to kill you on the show."

Kit shrugs and comes up with a wince that Jesse sees is a smile filtered through pain. Kit lives by a rigid code of not doing anything that would change Rhonda's appearance. She can't gain more than a few pounds without getting called on the carpet, can't change her shade of blond without a conference. When someone gets a great idea to go ice skating or ride the Wild Mouse at an amusement park, Kit has a low-key way of ducking out. She takes no chances, and has taken none for so long that she is immune to the impetuous gesture. And so Jesse knows that what she did in the backyard took the full complement of consequence into account. This information is both thrilling and unsettling. It means that Kit is someone quite other than Jesse has been able to imagine.

Dr. Thoms says her hand will be all right down the line. He called in a specialist from Jeff City who stitched the two blown-off tips back on. The palm is burnt, and Rhonda will have to be vampy and seductive while wearing a big bandage for a while, but in the end she should be back to her former, fully digited self. For the moment though, she is drugged and tranquil in the little room overlooking the hospital parking lot.

"My hero," Jesse says, holding on to the other hand.

"Sleepy," Kit says, and drops off like an infant.

Jesse sits silently for a while, and then Hallie comes in and settles heavily into the other chair and pulls out a complicated argyle sock she's knitting. At first Jesse thinks she's going to come up with something profound and serious, a soothing aphorism maybe. Hallie waits about two beats, then gestures toward Kit with her knitting. "What a show-off."

Jesse's eyes widen, then tear over and then she begins laughing in a helpless, shaking way. Hallie doesn't even crack a smile; she's as deadpan as Groucho. Kit wakes briefly. "What's so funny?"

Jesse leans over and brushes Kit's hair back with her hand, then eyeballs Hallie, and asks, "Can you give Kit some more local color? She thinks New Jerusalem is so sweet. You know. She loves the Frock Shop, the Noon Hour Cafe."

Jesse can see this request puts Hallie into a small quandary. She hates being thought of as quaint. She's always touting all the recent changes that have come to New Jerusalem. Three Oaks Mall. Paddock Towers under construction downtown. That Alice's new, trendy restaurant, whatever it's called. Even the franchises, which make her feel the town hasn't been passed by.

But these aren't the sorts of things Kit wants to hear. Her eyes are bright with anticipation through the druggy glaze. She wants quaint, and because Jesse wants Kit to be happy, and because Hallie wants Jesse to have whatever she wants, she puts her sock and needles in her lap and says to Kit, "Perhaps your girlfriend has failed to show you Betty's Button Hut?"

As she smiles, Kit's eyes flutter a while, then close.

Hallie sighs and settles back into the chair, looking around. "The last time you and I were in this crummy place together was when you got these stitches out." She reaches up toward Jesse, who is standing over the bed, and traces the small, deep, right-angle scar along her jaw line.

Jesse puts her own hand to it. "This? You know, I don't even remember how I came by it."

"I don't know how you could have forgotten. I remember it as if it just happened. We were out swimming at the country club — your mother and me and you and Willie. You were only seven or eight. You weren't a swimmer yet, just a kid fooling around in the pool. It was late in the afternoon.

"Your mother and I were tanning on side-by-side chaises longues. She was using me as a wind blind, lighting up a cig.

I looked up and saw you. You'd shot up into the air above that old, sprung diving board, and were trying to unfold yourself from a jackknife, but you weren't fast enough, or you hadn't dove out far enough. I don't know. Something. On the way back down, you hit the corner of the board. You sliced down through the water, making this cloudy little trail of red behind you.

"I just went nuts, I guess. I jumped in — forgot about my extra pounds and my terrycloth beach jacket and the small problem of not knowing how to swim a stroke. I was in there before the lifeguard was even off his perch. Dragged you up and out and put you in the back seat of my car."

"That two-tone car, cream and — "

"Brown, yes indeed. So you do remember after all. We went to Doc Wemby's office, do you remember that? He sewed up your face while I held on to your hand, which I remember as being very hot, while you — you were always such a tough little thing — you just stared straight ahead."

Some moments supersaturate, take on almost more than one tiny fragment of time can hold. How, Jesse thinks, can you hold this sort of memory of someone and at the same time just try to seem normally, regularly, pleased when she comes to visit for a few days every few years?

"Did we really go to Doc's office?" Jesse says. "What I remember is being at your house and he was there. Maybe it was a Sunday and he wasn't at his office? I can see him putting my stitches in on that giant old sofa you used to have. I was watching TV. Some show with singing mice."

"I thought you didn't remember this at all," Hallie says.

"I didn't. But now I remember the part about the stitches and the singing mice."

Hallie looks like she is about to say something, then

reaches down and tugs loose a length of crimson yarn. She catches Jesse looking down at the gnarled socks, suppressing a smile, and says, "Be nice to me or I'll give you these for Christmas."

They sit in silence for a while, then Hallie goes down the hall, "for a smoke." When she's gone, Jesse sits and watches Kit, who, sleeping and bandaged and so vulnerable in both of these aspects, elicits in Jesse a hard-to-gather-up constellation of emotions. She leans in to kiss her lover, who stirs from sleep just enough to vaguely kiss back. It's a goofy, muddled, private moment, which, Jesse sees when she looks toward the door of the room, has been witnessed by Laurel Owen, who is clearly nonplussed, and holding a bouquet of helium-filled balloons.

"It was just so awful," Laurel says, trying to regroup, holding the balloons out to Jesse. "The accident, I mean. I thought I'd — "

Jesse gets up and welcomes her, and they pass back and forth between them the necessary questions and answers about the stitches and the hand and the prognosis, but through these Jesse can see Laurel isn't coming down any. Standing there in the doorway, she was presented with too much information all at once. There's no way for Jesse to go back and fill in the blanks in an orderly progression. Laurel has already hardened from the inside, Jesse can feel it. She is now here only until the first possible moment she can leave, go home, and tell her husband and the two sisters she's close to, but probably (after a brief internal debate) not her mother.

Sometimes this still happens. Because of the life Jesse lives, and the tolerant strip of territory she inhabits, she almost never runs into it anymore. When it does happen, it's always in surprising ways, from unexpected directions. A cleaning woman who quit abruptly in a burst of Spanish Jesse didn't understand, but of course did. The new poetry instructor who made a dinner date to "network" with Jesse, and then, a few days later, called to cancel with some excuse peculiar enough that Jesse got the drift.

Even with so much time passing between these sorts of events, they always clip her, and then make her sorry for herself, and then for the person locked in place against her, and then for everyone, for the benighted planet. Now, though, she has only gotten to the part where she's sorry she and Laurel won't be able to catch up with each other and find a little bit of their old coloring book camaraderie.

Laurel is long gone by the time Hallie comes back. Jesse is thinking and stretching, hands pressing out against the window frame.

"Get out for a while," Hallie tells her. "I'll spell you for a bit."

"But — "

"Go for a swim."

Jesse walks from the hospital, past her mother's house, where she picks up a bathing suit, then heads toward the three-block stretch that constitutes downtown New Jerusalem. She goes past the bronze revolving door of the Fricke Building, where Hallie has her Harper Method parlor, then farther along stops in front of the drugstore. The ancient neon sign still reads AUSTIN DRUGS, although it has been more than twenty years since her father owned it.

She presses against the glass of the door. Once inside, she is instantly overwhelmed. It's the smell of the place, exactly the same as the summer she worked here, when she was sixteen. The summer before everything changed.

 As soon as swim practice was over, Jesse was expected to come straight over here. Her father thought part-time jobs built character. He was big in Junior Achievement.

 Jesse is surprised to see the soda fountain still there. An older woman — she thinks it might be Louise Gates, who used to be ticket taker at the Vogue movie theater — is having a Coke and a grilled cheese sandwich, with a flutter of potato chips and two dill pickle slices at the edge of the plate. The counter girl is someone she doesn't recognize, an earnest-looking girl.

 Jesse can remember standing exactly where the girl is now, shooting cherry syrup into the bottom of a Coke glass and suddenly she'd hear her father's voice come booming up from the back of the store. Fitting some old guy for a truss. Or giving directions on how to apply drawing salve to boils. Announcing the importance of roughage in the battle against constipation. Embarrassing her so much the tops of her ears heated up and turned red. She closed her eyes and wished him into silence. And then he died, suddenly, terribly — embarrassing even in death — crumpling inside his tuba in the Fourth of July parade. Collapsing onto the asphalt of Sycamore Street, leaving Jesse with a bundle of feelings she has never been able to square the corners on, tie up with a single string.

She has gold-plated keys to both her training pools, the one out at the country club and the one at the high school, both given to her after her parade. "Thank you, Mr. Masso," she said to Louis Masso, who was the mayor then. Now he's dead so many years. He shot himself the day he found out he had bone cancer. But this was the summer of 1968, and he was still alive and hugely fat, and Jesse was seventeen and in the center of her big moment, absorbing the spotlight as though it were afternoon sun. She read from the damp, scribbled speech in her hand.

"I accept this key to the James Monroe High School pool with deep appreciation, and some sense of the appropriateness of the gift. Probably no one in the history of the pool has spent quite as many hours in it as I have. As Coach Trembley once said to me at the end of a long, long practice [nod at Coach T.], 'Jesse — I do believe you've worn that poor water out' [wait for possible laughter]."

She still keeps the gold keys on her ring for good luck. Today, inside the school, the halls are dark and she can't remember where the light switch is. She pushes open the door marked GIRLS LOCKER and walks between the rows of tan metal. She has been here before in recent years and so it's not a total shot of past. More like an oldie that has come up on the radio enough times to start having a life of its own, disconnected from any direct buzzers.

Jesse got into swimming by a fluke of ability, as opposed to an interest pursued. It was just one of the alternatives in a mandatory phys ed program. In sixth grade the choices were swimming or calisthenics. She hated the idea of shinnying up ropes and vaulting stationary horses, and so took swimming even though it would mean getting her hair wet. That she turned out to be any good at it surprised her as much as it did anyone else.

She got little encouragement from her mother, who thought all sports were ridiculous. Her father's interest she squelched early on when he turned up with ancient books on swim technique, an absurd-looking rubber cap he'd ordered for her through the Harper Method catalogs, a flesh-colored item that promised to protect the scalp from the hazards of chlorine. She had to keep him away from this part of her life, or he would take it over, throw it off balance.

While it was a relief to be involved in something that didn't center on Willie, Jesse knew there was only so far she could get in swimming on her own. Beyond a certain point, there was no one in the area to coach her. She'd have to hook up with someone at the state university, or better yet, from one of the training camps or big swimming schools in Florida or California. But this would take money, which, in the family of a high school English teacher and a small-town druggist with a retarded child in special programs and schools, was in short supply.

And then out of the blue, Doc Wemby stepped forward with generous and continuing checks. She has always marveled that he did this, what with five kids of his own, including Keith, the Korean boy he and his wife had adopted. It was a curious thing about Doc, how much he turned out to love swimming.

Jesse hangs her pants and T-shirt on the broken hooks inside the locker and pulls on a racing suit so chlorine-corroded only the seams are anywhere near blue. It's a Bellini Jesse Austin model. She still has a boxful in her closet, a gift from the company.

She thinks of Tom Bellini and the promotion tour for this suit — greeting girls in swimwear departments, making her speech ("Open a New Window") in high school auditoriums, retreating from Tom's hotel room advances, writing letters to Marty down in Australia, determinedly light in tone, desperate in content. The tour ended in New York, which seemed so much like where she should be that she felt already home. It wouldn't be necessary to go on, back to New Jerusalem. And so she lived for a time on her money from the tour plus a cashed-in plane ticket, while she pressed the Olympic committee to press Columbia to let her in on scholarship.

She grabs her towel, slams the wiggling locker door shut, and heads through the doorway under the sign TO POOL.

This pool has been claimed by Jesse's past, both inside her, and in the larger reality. It is, of course, the scene of much varsity and junior varsity practice, lifesaving and scuba lessons, weekend Gym 'n' Swim. And on Saturday nights, in a subterranean tradition passed down through the years, high school couples who know their way around sometimes sneak in by diving naked off the balcony. But to the side of all this, the pool also holds a large part of its identity as the pool where Jesse Austin trained. There's a plaque, but it's more than that.

Still, when she comes into it, everything this particular pool calls up is overwhelmed by its universal poolness. It is all pools everywhere, beckoning to her. *Pssst.* The air dulled with overheating and chlorine, the sounds sharpened by reflective acoustics. Footfalls slap, rubber caps snap like toy pistols, flat bodies detonate against flat water.

Jesse gets up on a middle-lane starting block, pushes the balls of her feet into the sandpaper surface, tongues her goggles and pulls them on, then bears down, to somewhere beneath reverie, where, if all the circumstances are right, she can — for an instant — feel it all over again.

She leaps. Arms thrown in front of her, hurtling over the first ten feet or so in midair, then slamming into the water. From there she takes it with S-strokes, starting with hand in front of head, swooping out to the side, then bringing it back, close to the hip. Aquaphysics. The point being to push against still, rather than already moving, water.

At the far end, she rolls into a flip turn and heads back. When her hand slaps the wall, it feels like a pretty good time, but isn't. She won't know for sure. She never clocks herself now. She doesn't want to spend the rest of her life racing against someone she needs not to be anymore. Or racing against a Marty Finch who is unavailable for revision, standing always unreachable at the horizon. Always eighteen, laughing wildly, high on the oxygen of her own promise.

She wonders how much of her travel in the underpasses of her subconscious have been an attempt to get back to a girl who stopped existing in the precise way Jesse remembers her the day after Jesse last saw her, the day at the airport with stolen kisses in the ladies' room, then cousinly hugs in the terminal, promises whispered with warm breath. Letters — they would write a flurry of them. "I'll peel off the stamps and carry them in my mouth," Marty said. "To taste you on the back."

They would find their way back to each other. What were a couple of hemispheres to them? This was just the beginning.

And of course, it was simply the end. The last Jesse saw of Marty Finch was that morning in the airport, just before they made dashes for departure gates at opposite ends of the terminal, to board planes headed for opposite corners of the world. Jesse wrote, Marty didn't. Not even so much as a nervous letter pretending to forget everything, to revise their tiny history into a passing friendship. Nothing. It was like a wall had dropped down into the ocean between them, a great barrier reef holding their lives separate, not touching, on either side of it. This is the part Jesse can't stand to go over, the part that doesn't come with any color.

She walks back through town to the hospital. Hallie is still there. Plus Jesse's mother, who has brought William. They've also brought Kit a sack from the Burger King.

"I was here for my female troubles," Frances says. "I know how bad the food is. It got so I'd throw up just from hearing the cart rattling down the hall."

Everything has been pulled inside out. Kit is now the most wonderful person in the world. And the injured party. She has seen the worst of this place. Amends must be made.

William sits quietly in a green vinyl armchair in the corner. No one knows if he understands what happened, or not.

The next day, when they let Kit out, Darrell takes her and Jesse up into the hills, where he knows some quilting women. He haggles a good price for Kit on the one she wants, maize and Wedgwood blue with purple dogs in odd squares. Through all this Kit is attentive and appreciative and a little fuzzy from the Percodan.

"They'll make you a sexy bandage on the show," Jesse says in the van on the way back to town. "Everything'll be okay."

Kit nods, but Jesse can see she's not convinced.

Jesse's mother stands in the drive on Wednesday morning while they get a horribly late start, running back into the house three or four times for stuff they've forgotten, and then finally they pull out with Kit and Jesse's mother waving and Jesse driving and waving until they turn the corner. They slip out of town the back way. Kit wants a scenic route.

Out on the highway, the high grass shimmers with the heat coming off it while they are packed in air conditioning. They pass the big billboard for Pratt's Caverns. Kit says should they stop? Jesse shakes her head. "It's just a corny old sight. Really."

"Last chance," Kit points to the LAST CHANCE! billboard for the cave, with a cutout representation of its stalactite xylophone.

Hours later, around Dayton, they approach the junction of I-70 and I-75. A round-cornered green sign reads:

LEFT TWO LANES—NEW YORK
RIGHT TWO LANES—FLORIDA

"We could take the wrong turnoff," Kit says. "I wouldn't have to face Decker, or my agent. Everyone's going to be sweet as pie for ten seconds, then they're going to kill me. Florida's nice, isn't it? We could open an orange juice stand. Sell O.J. and coconut shakes."

"The thing is," Jesse says, as the sign flips into the immediate forgotten past, "my mother needs for me — for us — to take William for a while."

She holds her breath, listening to the light pinging of the rental car's out-of-tune engine, fearing Kit's response. But there are only a few seconds of silence before she says, "No problem."

And then, "Can we stop tonight at that Jailhouse Motel we saw on the way out?"

6s & 7s & 9s

THEY'RE SITTING in the parking lot behind the Venus Beach police station. Even though there is a smoky storm rolling in from low over the ocean, Jesse unlatches and buzzes down the top on the ancient, silver-blue Cadillac Eldorado — the Boss Hog. She needs to get some air into the situation. She's feeling spontaneously combustible, her first-line reaction to Anthony.

He's sitting in the other wide bucket seat, emoting No Problem. Jesse knows this posture is defensive deep cover for some roiling tumble of nervousness and fear and self-doubt. She has read books and books on dealing with the difficult adolescent and knows this is a critical moment when she should help him out, say something maternal and supportive. The best she can come up with, though, is, "You really fucked up this time."

He reaches over with his good hand to turn on the radio. Wilson Phillips joins them from the dashboard. These girls are having troubles of their own. They're pleading in wire-tight harmony to make someone — baby, baby — understand he's got to release them.

Jesse has two simultaneous lines of conversation with Anthony. One is the wry but kindly set of responses she means to come up with. (Sally Field would play her in the heartwarming movie version of her relationship with Anthony.) The other is made up of what comes out of her mouth whenever she is actually pressed up against the enormous stupidity of his life, and his studied lack of affect around it.

Last night, he got caught liberating the stereo from a BMW parked behind the Harbor View restaurant. The cops came in with their lights cut. Anthony panicked and ripped his hand open on the teeth of the hole he'd just made in the dash. He has spent the past several hours in the Orange Grove Hospital emergency room, then at the arraignment, then cooling his heels in the Venus Beach lockup until Jesse could get over to the bank and make bail. Now he's studying his bandage, pressing at it where a watery red is seeping through.

When Anthony was little, Jesse used to sit at the beach with other young mothers and wonder if they all envied her. He was so full of surprises. Drawings he'd crayon of the inhabitants of his imagination — a man made of water, a friendly animal so furry he'd keep a boy warm through the coldest night in the wilderness. Tunes played on a harmonica picked up in a playground trade. Later, magic shows with labor-intensive tricks, scarves pried out of fists, coins found behind ears, but only after a heartbreaking amount of searching.

And then somewhere along the way, he slipped from surprises into secrets, started becoming this elaborately unknowable person. Which makes Jesse crazy. She sits quietly next to him and wants to tear him open and crawl inside, find out who the hell is in there.

He's pulling up the bandage now, peering underneath. He sees her look over, and shrugs. "Everybody's a geek when you come down to it."

He is sitting as far away as possible, hugging the door, looking more eleven than nineteen. He punches two buttons on the radio and gets them away from Jesse's Top 40 station, to easy listening.

Jesse thinks he must be fooling around. "Like being in an elevator, only going forward," she says.

"It's a pretty good station," he says. Anthony will defend anything Jesse attacks. It's pure reflex now.

Then, in the middle of nothing, the windshield wipers start up again. They do this quite often lately, and then shut off again, on their own. It doesn't seem worth taking the car in for. If Jesse is at a light and someone is staring, she just squirts some bluejuice so it looks like she's cleaning the glass. Anthony wheels the volume up a little on the radio to cover the sound of dragging rubber blades. He looks out at the city beach. Jesse glances over and sees it's empty of humans in the face of the approaching storm. There is a large flock of gulls on one patch, utterly still and all pointed toward the sea.

Anthony's station is now playing a lilting instrumental version of "Hotel California."

"I met a couple of interesting guys in there," he says.

"*Precisely* why you should always try to get into the best jails. So you'll be able to make those important career contacts."

She doesn't know how this happens. She sits blank-faced, determined to be impassive when Anthony says something idiotic. Then Anthony says something idiotic and a switch inside her flips and she is suddenly talk show host to his dopey guest, riffing on whatever he has just said, rolling her eyes innocently and saying something that makes the audience go up for grabs, makes Ed McMahon pull off his glasses to wipe away the tears of laughter. But there is no audience in the car, no Ed. Just Anthony, disappearing into himself as he always does when he's made to play straight man, and Jesse, once again shorting out a connection she pretty desperately wants.

She tacks around now, tries to pull things back into a more manageable past. "You want to come home? Spend a night or two with me and Sharon? We can make BLTs. Play Risk."

"Oh," he says, and then pauses so long Jesse thinks this is all he's going to say. But then he adds, "I think Lynette is probably expecting me."

The thick sky has been holding rain for most of the afternoon, which now finally begins sifting down in light starter drops. Jesse looks over to see if he wants the top up, but he shakes his head. "I won't melt." And so they drive the rest of the way like this — top down, wipers flapping — objects of curiosity to people in other cars passing them by.

Anthony has been living with Lynette in a trailer out by the old Seminole reservation for about a year. They met at Long John Silver's, where she is assistant manager and he's a counter representative.

Lynette has dogs, two of them, a special kind of poodle. She and Anthony drive a beat-up station wagon rigged with wire carriers in the back. They go around Florida, sometimes up to Georgia or Alabama on long weekends, to shows where these dogs win ribbons. They stay in motels, which, amazingly, let in hundreds of these owner-dog combos. There's some kind of social life around all this. Anthony says it's fun. Of course a lot of what's fun in his book is enhanced by boutique drugs and wine coolers.

A few months back, when he had been living with Lynette for a while, Jesse cleaned out Anthony's old closet. On a high shelf she found a row of paperbacks. She didn't think he ever read. But these books were puffy, soft and fat from handling. Texts. They were all from the same series, "Adventures at Whitefish Bay." The covers were *Argosy*-like illustrations of the world within, a place populated with rough and ready guys. Lumberjacks and fishermen and miners, guys who "topple the big trees, bring in the big fish and pan for the big gold." Clint and Buck and Thor. They might "settle scores with their fists," but they are always there to help a buddy, even "at the risk of life and limb." At night they head home to Eskimo girlfriends, devoted women who fix large meals of elk steaks and mashed potatoes.

Since coming upon these books, Jesse's worries have downshifted. For years, she imagined something jittery and dangerous behind the wall of Anthony. Now she thinks the truth is more likely that although he has a complex, colorful inner life, it's complex and colorful and banal. A biblical epic movie, a View-Master travelog.

This leaves her with absolutely nothing to do. She can't go to Plan B. She can't send out deprogrammers if Anthony is not on some program, if he has only shuffled off — away, but to no place in particular. When she tries to reach for him, to bring him back, it's all slick, flat surface. She can't find anyplace to grab on to. Except during these rescue missions, when the phone rings in the middle of the night after he has been picked up — high, usually in peculiar circumstances. Building a giant pyramid of oranges from fruit shaken down in someone's grove. Spray-painting graffiti on the two buses that make up the Venus Beach public transportation system.

This is their only time together anymore. Because he's in a weakened state, messed-up and full of vague regret, he usually lets Jesse bring him home. She turns the shower on full blast and holds his wasted, marked-up body in front of the spray, turned to as cold as you can get water to run down here. She lets her love for him show while he can't notice. Then when he has resurfaced, she gets out towels and talks to him pointlessly about getting into some job or schooling that won't leave him at such loose ends. Computers or hairstyling. She's just punting. She really has no idea what the answers are for Anthony.

In a weird way, this incident, an actual crime, seems almost an improvement. There is an obvious point to boosting a radio. She can say to herself, to Elaine Kurczak over coffee, "My son's a criminal, Anthony's been led astray by a criminal element." There is a definable problem. Until now, the trouble he has gotten into has been vague — foolish statements nobody else gets.

With a real problem, though, he is beyond her gestures of salvation. This time love won't be enough; money will be necessary. Anthony used his first call to phone his dad, Jesse's ex-husband, Tom Bellini, who is now going to come down from New York. Mighty Mouse to save the day. This depresses Jesse nearly as much as Anthony's troubles.

*

The rain starts really hammering down as they drive into the mobile home park. She pulls in alongside his trailer, under the striped aluminum car canopy. Anthony helps her wrestle the top up, then asks if she wants to come in and dry off. "We have a towel," he says, opening the screen door, pushing the overexcited-to-see-him dogs back inside with his knee.

Inside, the TV is on, but between channels. Lynette is there, but not really at home to company. She is kneeling on the floor next to the open Hide-a-Bed, her upper body facedown across it. There's a lot of underside to their life-style. Jesse has found it generally pays to call first before dropping by.

"I guess she's napping," Anthony says lamely, and drops to the floor next to her, smoothing her rumpled hair with his bandaged hand. She doesn't stir. In repose, Lynette looks — and Jesse can't believe she missed this until now — amazingly Eskimo-ish.

It's dusk when the Boss Hog — wipers flapping away although the storm is long past, back seat loaded with plastic pump barrels of chlorine treatment, fresh speeding ticket stuck in the visor — pulls through the pink and green portals of the Bud Barris Swim Academy, a small compound with stucco walls surrounding the pool, two locker-shower rooms, an office, and attached at the back by a breezeway, a three-bedroom bungalow where Jesse lives, now just with her daughter, Sharon.

When Jesse and Tom bought this school (built in the forties by Barris himself, the great backstroker), it had been through a couple of halfhearted rehabilitations, then had just been sitting abandoned for years. The contractor suggested changing the name and pulling down the corny Hollywood portals, another punch line in this comic landscape of windmilled miniature golf courses and buzzing go-cart tracks and, down the highway a bit, the giant Lucky Whip can. But Tom prevailed. He was at that moment full of notions of possibility. Freshly married, their first baby on the way, Jesse just stepping down from the Olympics. He saw the portals as a fairy-tale entrance to what would surely be a wonderful chain of events.

Now, all these years later, Tom is gone, that first baby a miscarriage she almost never thinks about anymore, the Olympics something that happened to another person, someone she knows well enough and remembers fondly, but not quite her. And once again, the portals are in sad need of paint and replastering. Even here in Venus Beach, which is not so much a place as a franchise opportunity, a dot on the giant connect-the-dots map of Pizza Huts and Gaps and Wal-Marts, even here where there is never that much happening, people still have jazzier ways to spend their leisure time than going back and forth in a rectangle of water.

Jesse is trying to turn things around with enterprise and innovation. She is constantly working on new ideas. She has had some small success renting the pool out for splash parties. She does these with her friend Elaine, who manages the Pancake Haus in town and runs a free-lance catering business on the side.

Jesse has also livened up the school's schedule with several new programs. A Scared to Death class for adults who have always been too frightened to get in the water. And Tuesday afternoons, Sharon leads a large group of the elderly through Aquarobics for Arthritics. This doesn't really make money because Jesse has to crank the pool heater up so high, but the old folks really enjoy it. The pool is packed. It's nice to see.

Sharon has been holding down the fort all day, is alone in the pool as Jesse comes in. She stands in the shadows and watches. The underwater lights are on, and so a wavy, lurid turquoise floats up against the deep red roses and the terra cotta pool wall and beyond them, a milky pink sunset that has followed the storm. Sharon is a cigarette boat, a high rider through the water. Her freckled shoulders clear the surface by several inches. When she used to do sprint work, she was breathtaking.

A couple of years back, when she beat Jesse at a hundred meters, Jesse thought maybe the baton was passing. If it happened, it would have to be Sharon who took it. When the kids were little, Jesse had thought Anthony would be the one. At three, while Sharon was still splashing around in the baby pool, Anthony was already jumping off the high dive and wiggling his little body the full length of the lap pool.

But then he hit adolescence and figured out he could get at Jesse by staying out of the water. He began to, and still does, go sullen at so much as the suggestion of swimming, a rejection Jesse minds more than she can account for. By the time he got out of the water, though, Sharon was getting in, and Jesse could transfer her hopes. After Sharon had done well in a few high school meets her first year on the team, Jesse began to think about getting her into Sea Breeze down in Pompano, where Jesse herself trained for those last months before she went to the nationals.

But it was a hope that didn't bear too much close examination, given how confined Jesse had felt, having to train through nearly her whole adolescence. The only thing she could have been wishing for, really, was a replication of her own chance, one she could this time not blow, an erasure of her own failure with her daughter's success. When she realized this, it made her feel terribly small.

At any rate, it doesn't look like this is going to happen. Sharon has the intelligence of technique and enough perseverance to blot up the monotony. What she has lost as she has come into the prime of her adolescence are the insane levels of desire required. Becoming a world-class athlete is simply no longer very important to her. At seventeen, Sharon's desires have irised down to a sequence of guys from her school who, one after another, are not calling her.

Now her best friend, Janine, is going with one of these guys, which has sent Sharon into a summer-long torpor. Most of the time she seems terribly low, as though she is on some medication of misery. Depressants. Even when she swims now, there's a brooding, urgent cast to it, as though she is boring through the water, escaping the landed world where her sorrow awaits her.

Nights she stays back in her room, enclosed in her Walkman, searching *Glamour* and *Seventeen* for secret passages into the affections of whichever boy is responsible for the current coma of the phone. Jesse wishes she could just call Don Corleone to help Sharon out. The don would send a couple of soft-spoken, extremely reasonable guys in beautifully cut suits over to this boy's — Ian's — house. These guys would explain the situation to Ian in a soft-spoken, reasonable way, and if he didn't come around, dead fishes and horse heads would turn up. Ian's thoughts on the subject would gain a new clarity, and he would dump Janine and call Sharon.

Sharon's teenage dilemmas are both like and not at all like Jesse's. Janine, for instance, already has a baby, Madonna, named, of course, after Madonna. She had the baby at the end of the school year, won't say who the father is, but Ian is sure it's him, and this has made him hostage to Janine, who seems not to care about him one way or the other. Before the baby, Ian and Sharon had been dating. Now Sharon says, "Maybe they weren't really dates."

Coming out of her flip turn now, Sharon sees Jesse and swims up to the side, pulling off her goggles. "Hey. How'd it go?" She always sounds calm, even when she's agitated, which Jesse knows she is now, about Anthony.

"The hand. They don't know yet. Everything else — the situation — is a mess. He called in sick at the fish shop, but when they see that hand, I don't know. I dropped him at the trailer. Such an upbeat atmosphere. Did you ever notice, by the way, how much Lynette looks like an Eskimo?"

"Mom, she's blond. I think she's even Swedish, isn't she? I mean, her name is Swenson."

"Still," Jesse says.

"I was worried they'd keep him in," Sharon says. "That he'd freak out. You know how claustrophobic he is." Jesse didn't know. She knows most of what she knows about Anthony now through Sharon.

"He's just out on bail," Jesse says. "There's a hearing scheduled for Friday. But your father knows a guy — 'turbo lawyer' — who's supposed to smooth it all over before it comes to that. Of course, this is great for Anthony, but still, it makes me a little queasy that your father is going to just walk in and stuff the situation full of his money and make it right again."

"Come on, lighten up. Don't get global. I'll fix some dinner," Sharon says, hoisting herself out of the pool, tying a towel around her waist, bending to twist another around her hair. She shuts down the pool lights and takes Jesse's hand as they start through the breezeway that leads into the house. Inside, she pulls on some shorts and starts up dinner while Jesse pulls a couple of apricots out of the vegetable bin in the refrigerator, then falls into the one-armed recliner they've pulled into the kitchen. She sticks to its plastic upholstery. The compressor on their aging air conditioner is no match for the heat and humidity of this summer.

"I may need a lawyer myself. Some dweeb motorcycle cop pulled me over this afternoon. Someone new. They're doing radar from planes now, so we can all throw away our fuzz busters, I guess."

"Oh, Ma, you can't get any more points!"

"Don't worry. I'm planning on being incredibly slow from now on. People walking will pass me by."

"Don't spoil your appetite," Sharon says, eyeing the apricots. She turns back to the counter. "I'm going gourmet tonight." She drops a couple of hash brown patties into the toaster slots and goes into an off-camera, "Lifestyles of the Rich and Famous" narration: "One of Florida's maverick young chefs, Bellini is bodacious with her use of frozen toaster foods."

"You going out tonight?" Jesse says.

Sharon turns and nods and rolls her eyes like a maniac. "To the show with Janine and the baby. Ian's meeting us there."

"She brings the baby to the movies? Doesn't that drive everyone nuts?"

"Nah. Mostly she sleeps. Mostly I hold her while I pretend I'm watching the movie, but really I get to drive myself crazy looking out of the side of my eye to see if Janine and Ian are making out, or worse."

"What worse?" Jesse says, and Sharon rolls her eyes again, this time a slow, "get real" roll.

"Well," Jesse says. "It'll probably be character-building."

"You don't have to say stuff like that."

"I don't, do I? I keep thinking I do, but I suppose I really don't. Sometimes you don't know what to do, being a parent, so you just mouth some worthless thing your own mother said to you." She sees from behind that Sharon has stopped in the middle of her flurry of cooking motions, her shoulders are shuddering softly, and so knows without seeing tears that Sharon is crying. This happens so suddenly lately, like the brief afternoon rains down here.

She can't bear her daughter's suffering; she feels it too acutely. Sharon knows this, which makes her feel guilty on top of depressed. The two of them get tangled up in the looping lariats of each other's feelings. Jesse has to get her out of here. Sharon has one more year of high school, then Jesse is going to make sure she goes away to college. *Way* away. Otherwise she fears they'll turn into some horrifying mother-daughter duo. Alluding cryptically to family secrets, dwelling obsessively on ancient memories. Behaving oddly when visitors stop by.

"Hey," she says to Sharon's back now. "Just stay home if you want."

It will be better for Jesse, though, if Sharon goes out. Then Jesse can slip off and pay Oscar a visit, which she would really like to do. She hates to twirl out of the house like Gidget while her daughter stays home, despondent for lack of a boyfriend.

But Sharon has something else pressing on her mind tonight. Jesse can tell. The tone of her depression is slightly different. Jesse waits.

"Do you think we could get some new furniture?" Sharon asks in a damp voice. "A camelback sofa, maybe."

"Oh no," Jesse says, seeing that this is about Tom.

"I only don't want him to think we've gone downhill," Sharon says.

"I'll have to remember to put my teeth in on Thursday."

"No, I mean" — Sharon turns from the stove and waves with a big fork in her hand — "you may have noticed how few kitchen tables in magazines are covered with lime green contact paper. Or how when Barbara Walters interviews celebrities in their homes, the chairs always have two arms. *Both* chairs. The celebrities never have to say to Barbara, 'Here. You take the good chair.' "

"It's not like we have a dead washing machine on the front porch," Jesse says.

"No. That's Alabama tacky. We're Florida shabby."

Jesse pushes the lever forward, launching herself slowly out of the recliner. She lays out plates and forks and paper napkins and a big plastic bottle of Coke on the coffee table in front of the TV.

Sharon brings out the hash browns and a pan of scrambled eggs. "*Au fromage,*" she says, indicating the slices of cheese melted on top of the eggs. "Bellini's genius lies in elevating the humble to the sublime, as in her breakthrough dessert, Ho Hos Suzette."

They turn on "Wheel of Fortune."

"But, can Vanna handle the pressure tonight?" Sharon says.

They've noticed that although Vanna White is required to say only "bye bye," a lot of nights lately she's been dropping her second "bye."

Two hours later, Sharon is out at the Quad Cinemas at the Fashion Mall, and Jesse is lying on the low tides of Oscar's water bed, the first purchase of his new bachelorhood. When his wife, Louise, left, she took with her a van full of their regular sensible furniture and the next day Oscar went over to Water Bed World and, not on drugs or anything, let himself be talked into this California king with gray marbleized Formica frame and urn-shaped lamps attached to the nightstands. The only thing he didn't take was the fountain option.

The TV's on, a PBS special on an old Hollywood director. Clips of his movies, and then little interviews with stars who worked with him, now terrifically old. Most of them look like they were exhumed for the occasion.

"If they ever do a salute to you," Jesse tells Oscar, "I won't appear on it. I couldn't stand for everyone to see me so decrepit and dressing like I haven't been out of the house since 1958. I'll phone in my little testimonial."

Oscar is across the room, posing in front of the mirror on the closet door in Jesse's cotton camisole, which is stretched tight across his chest, thick black hairs corkscrewing out through the lace at the top. "I'll bet I could be great at drag, except I'd never get anything that fit. Probably all they have in my size is geriatric wear. Those girdles as long as bermudas. Underpants like cabanas." He comes back to bed and Jesse eddies a little on the rubberized seas.

"Come on. You'll stretch it out," she says, plucking at the camisole's spaghetti strap.

"Yes, but now it'll have my musk all over it. Oscar: The Fragrance."

She and Oscar have been lovers, or whatever it is they are but don't call themselves, for quite some time now. The five years she has been on her own and the last couple she was married to Tom. At first on the sly because they were both married. Even since they've become freed up, though, they haven't made any big changes. Now she parks in his driveway when she comes over, instead of around the block, is about all.

If they came out of this gray area, it would be into each other's lives. They'd feel obliged to go out to dinner together and celebrate little anniversaries. They'd have to begin some kind of complicated partnership instead of just hanging in with this low-maintenance thing. And too, they'd be forced to align themselves against the local brand of redneck hatred. Oscar is black, and Venus Beach is a place where enlightenment has pretty much caught on, but race relations are still a bit sticky in patches. Jesse would be willing to take on some trouble around this. She enjoys shaking small minds and listening to the beads rattle around inside. But Oscar isn't up for it. He says he just wants to sell Toyotas and watch Dolphins games and not wind up as the party torch on someone's front lawn.

The real issue for Jesse is that she doesn't want a big romantic deal with anyone around here. She's trying to lighten up her luggage so she can be ready to take the night bus out.

He traces a finger along the small, right-angle scar on her jaw, bothering her while she does her nails with a bottle of polish she swiped from Sharon.

"How'd you get this anyhow?" Oscar says. "Knife fight?"

She closes the bottle, sets it down, and touches the scar carefully, not wanting to smear the polish. "Back talk from a diving board."

He kisses her, then rolls over.

"Paint my toenails?" he says, stretching his long, thick-thighed leg across her lap.

"I might be able to get Anthony something at the dealership," he says as she takes his foot and begins. "Washing the used cars. Writing up the windshields. It'd be kind of like vandalism, so he might really get into it. And he could work his way up. That's the problem with working at that fish hut. No future."

"What would he write on the windshields?"

"Come on. RUNS NEW. ONE OWNER. HATES GAS. Baby, I could get you such a deal on a Corolla right now. I could do the financing and spread your payments over forever. You wouldn't even notice you were buying anything." This is an old conversation. It kills Oscar that she won't let him sell her a Toyota.

"You'd give me a trade-in on the Boss Hog?" Jesse says.

"The Hog we dump at night in the Everglades," he says. "Let the quicksand take her down."

The TV is on when Jesse gets home. Sharon and Janine are watching a rock video featuring some sexually menacing-looking guys in leather and studded collars and sweaty chests. Jesse doesn't suppose these can be wholesome images for teenage girls just figuring themselves out, but on the other hand, she can't imagine how she could even begin to monitor all the stuff in the air around Sharon. She just counts on her daughter being able to resist all that is false or corrupt, while she worries endlessly that Anthony will fall prey to the most worthless temptations of the culture. She worries she's replicating her own mother's brand of parenting, leaving the strong child to fend for herself while fighting a lifetime of battles on behalf of the weak one.

Little Madonna is lying on the sofa in her diaper. She's busy playing with her toes. Sharon and Janine seem to have incorporated the baby into their lives so easily it amazes Jesse. She tries to imagine having a baby now herself and feels a swoon of exhaustion pass through her just at the idea.

"Hallie called," Sharon says.

"I'm beat. I'll catch her tomorrow."

"No, she said call as late as you want, she'll be up watching a vampire movie at Grandma's. She wants to give you her flight time."

Jesse's godmother lives nearby, about ten miles up the coast. Acting on what seemed to be pure impulse, she moved down here a couple of years back. Jesse would have liked her to move in with them, but Hallie is accustomed to being by herself, and so she bought a small apartment in a retirement community, Golden Sands. There's a restaurant on the grounds, and the apartment has built-ins like microwaves and dishwashers and a buzzer in the bathroom that will bring help in a crisis.

"I'd never use it," Hallie told Jesse. "I couldn't stand anyone finding me bruised in the tub, or headfirst on the floor in front of the commode."

She loves the atmosphere of the place, which seems to Jesse to be concocted mostly of souped-up fun used as a means of distracting the residents from the fact that the reaper is gaining on them. Hallie is one of the younger women, and cuts a jaunty figure around the grounds riding a huge tricycle, which seems to embarrass her not at all.

She minds Florida only in the hottest, most humid, buggiest part of the summer, and so makes this the time of her annual visit back home. This year, though, from what Jesse hears, it has been hotter in Missouri than down here. Hallie is due back in a couple of days and Jesse will pick her up at the airport in Palm Beach. This call can really wait, but if Jesse puts it off, Hallie — who likes to get everything squared away, written down, her boarding pass preprinted, her special meal (low-salt) ordered ahead — will become unnecessarily agitated.

Jesse pulls a carton of chocolate milk from the refrigerator and brings it along with her over to the wall phone. "I want to drink your blood," she says when Hallie picks up on the other end. Jesse's mother will have already gone to bed.

"You can afford to be witty. You're not watching this. I'm going to have to sleep with the lights on."

"Give me your flight time. Honestly, I can't wait until you're back," Jesse says, and writes everything down, then says in a low voice, "I will be wearing a piñata and standing under the big clock."

She doesn't mention Anthony's troubles. Hallie is staying in Jesse's mother's house, is probably using the downstairs extension in the den. Frances is probably sound asleep, but still. Jesse doesn't want to take the risk of being eavesdropped on. Her mother doesn't need to know about Anthony's arrest.

"How'd the party go?" she asks instead. Her mother retired in June, after forty-plus years of teaching English at

the high school. Hallie and some other old friends collab-
orated on a celebration.

"Oh, it was a yardful. Persis Goudy, that old bag of wind,
gave a speech that made your mother sound like Mr.
Chips."

Jesse can't think of anything upbeat to say about her
mother's career other than that she's happy she managed to
avoid ever winding up in her English class.

"Here's something, though," Hallie says. "Your mother's
gone and got herself a beau."

"Oh my."

"She'll tell you herself in a bit, I expect," Hallie says. "I
think just yet she's a little shy about it."

"A romance? Mother? Is he a geezer?"

"What a thing to say! And he is especially not. For these
parts and our age group, he's quite a hunk. I'll give you
details . . . you know. Later."

"Polaroids?"

"Mmm. Videos."

"Can we not do a pink cake this time? Please?" Elaine
Kurczak brings over one of the gold plastic thermos pitch-
ers that fulfill the Pancake Haus's "bottomless cup of coffee" promise. Jesse is sitting in the back booth, which is
tacitly set aside for staff. It's eleven in the morning, past the
breakfast crowd, before lunch starts, and Elaine can take
out half an hour to go over the menu for a sweet sixteen
splash party they're doing next week.

"Anthony's got himself in deep shit again," Jesse says non
sequiturily, although since all her conversations with Elaine
are really just installments of the same long, running conversation, there are really no non sequiturs, no antecedents
left too far behind.

Elaine nods and listens to the grisly details while she stands over Jesse, turning her cup right side up onto its saucer and filling it to exactly one-quarter inch from the top, all in one smooth professional motion.

"And now Tom's coming down here, to the rescue. I hate when I have to see him," Jesse says. "The experience beats me up, reminds me of everything I usually manage to forget. I don't know why he doesn't mind seeing me, but he doesn't seem to. Maybe he's just smoother at looking like he doesn't mind. But then again, maybe he really doesn't. He doesn't have anything to hate me about. I get to hate him, though, because there I was, sick to death of him, but determined to stick it out, and then he up and left me. Plus he sprung it on me so fast I didn't realize until the dust settled that his leaving meant I was the one stuck with the life we'd made together while he was the one going on to a clean new slate. Argh. I just think of him and my hands get itchy. Like a strangler."

"He's just a blip on your radar screen," Elaine says. "He's nothing. He's something dumb you did when you were young. Like sleeping all night with your hair in rollers."

"I try to come up with any of the feelings I must have had when we were first married. The closest I can get is remembering how I used to like watching him wash our car, then massage it with Simoniz paste for a whole Sunday afternoon. I think I thought this was virile, or something. It doesn't seem nearly enough to marry somebody for, though. I think he was just a bad choice based on hazy motives.

"I know I must have been crazy about him, though, because there was this other guy, back home. Cute in a big bear sort of way. I'm not sure why I let him slip away. Probably I thought he was too nice, or too, well, 'back home.' I think I thought that with Tom everything would be different. Instead, it was the same, just in a different location."

She sweeps a hand through the air to include all of Venus Beach, like a model on a game show while the announcer describes the seven-piece living room suite the contestants might win.

"When I look back it seems like there was this short little span of time right after Mexico when I had to make all the crucial decisions in my life. Only I was way too young to do anything intelligent. I was younger than Anthony is now and he seems impossibly unformed to me. Barely beyond protoplasm."

"Criminal protoplasm," Elaine says. She gets to say stuff like this. Her own child is a Deadhead. The girl left three years ago — after Elaine put in seventeen years of hard, mostly single motherhood, several thousand dollars worth of orthodontia, private school tuition, and horseback riding lessons — to devote herself to following an aging hippie band.

"Most of what I did back then was just react, really," Jesse says. "My mother wanted me to go to college. Take English and teach, like she did. So of course I couldn't do that. She thought Tom was 'fly-by-night' and that clinched it. My path was clear."

"You should just be glad you've put him behind you," Elaine says. She has taken a seat opposite Jesse, and is pulling out a plastic cigarette, part of a three-hundred-dollar program that's her fourth shot at quitting. "Much better than the mess I've got with Steve. Just when I've pretty much forgotten him, he drops into the middle of some lonely night I'm having and gets me loaded on spumante and up to the Eros Motel, where they have that damn Tai-wanese basket."

"What do those rooms look like? I've always wondered."

"Oh, you know. Water beds and big-screen TVs with porno tapes. Brown shag everywhere. Every possible sur-face is carpeted, horizontal *and* vertical. And then he just disappears again and I'm left all riled up and confused."

"I don't know how you can have any confusion about Steve. He's living with a high school senior."

"She graduated."

Jesse doesn't let this even slow her down. "He drives that penis extender thing on truck tires. He goes to those pit bull matches. He's a nightmare. I hope you don't mind me saying this."

"No, I know."

Tessa, Elaine's second-shift cook, is standing over them now, a huge but extremely graceful black woman from some dot of an island in the Caribbean.

"I just need to know, are we keeping on the Stars and Stripes pancakes now that the holiday's past?"

Elaine thinks a moment. "Give it another week. People seem to enjoy a patriotic breakfast."

"What are . . . ?" Jesse says as Tessa drifts back into the kitchen like a float.

"Oh, you know. You top the cakes with blueberry and cherry compote, squirt lines of whipped cream between. Why don't you just tuck up with Oscar? He's so sweet. You could wait until Sharon's out of high school, then marry him and move north to one of those progressive cities where they ban guns and recycle everything and have gay mar-riages and black and white marriages, and are tolerant of everybody."

Jesse shakes her head and goes to pick up the creamer. In the process, she loses a strip of small hairs on her forearm to the tabletop's permanent coating of syrup. She tugs a napkin out of the dispenser, dips it in her water glass, and wipes the purple glue off her skin.

"Oscar and I've got a good thing, but it's an as-far-as-it-goes kind of thing. I'm trying to keep my options open while I'm looking for . . . I don't know. I don't know what I'm even looking for anymore. Some next thing, but I can't even imagine what it would be, really."

"At least I don't have illusions anymore," Elaine says. "At least I'm free of that. For me all that was over early. I knew everything else — even my marriages — would be downhill after . . . well, you know."

Elaine will never say the name directly. The most she'll say is The King. She hates to tell the story, which took place when she was sixteen in Detroit and Elvis was on tour and she was down near the front and when he slammed his guitar against his groin and sneered a little with his cruel lower lip, it was Elaine he sneered at, and immediately about twenty girls leapt on top of her and ripped off her charm bracelet and buttons from her jacket and pulled her nylons out of their garters and tore them to shreds. Second-class relics. Something belonging to someone Elvis had sneered at. Later, in back of the theater, one of Elvis's pack of guys asked Elaine and her friend Marilyn if they wanted to come to a party at the hotel, in Elvis's suite.

"How did he come on to you at the party? I mean, did he have a line, or did he just give you some sort of signal and you knew he wanted you to go to bed with him?"

Jesse, who thinks this is about the most fascinating thing that has ever happened to anyone she knows, always tries for a few more details on the rare occasions when the subject comes up. Usually Elaine guards the incident. Jesse thinks this is because she doesn't want to wear it out. Today, though, as she's flipping on the calculator so they can begin figuring what they've got to charge on the sweet sixteen party in order to turn a profit, she says, "He asked if I wanted to look at his coin collection."

The Hog is parked just outside the sliding glass doors of the baggage claim, in an area strictly forbidden with red and yellow stripes and several stern signs. A cop is looking the car over. Jesse rushes up, drops Hallie's bags, and bursts into an elaborate explanation. Hallie is an aged relative, the car had to be brought up close. She hopes Hallie, following a bit behind her, will get enough of the drift of this to look decrepit, and she does, stooping a bit, grabbing on to Jesse's arm with a quivering hand, allowing herself to be slowly folded into the passenger seat.

With the cop still glaring after them, Jesse slips into drive and pulls out in a restrained way, like a librarian behind the wheel of a bookmobile. By the time they get on the highway, though, she's up to the sort of speed that keeps her in a lively relationship with the Florida highway patrol.

Jesse looks over, sees Hallie is holding onto the glove compartment knob. She slows down a little.

"Did I miss anything?" Hallie says when Jesse has negotiated the swirl of exit lanes and they're headed in the right direction on Fed 1.

"Anthony's gotten himself in a spot of trouble," Jesse tells her. There won't be any way to keep the news from her, not with Tom coming down and all.

"He's just in that confusing patch," Hallie says when she

has heard the details. "Sorting through all the ways he can be until he gets to who he's going to become."

Jesse takes her eyes off the road long enough to look over at Hallie in amazement at her ability to put a good cast on even the worst situations when they involve Jesse or either of the kids. Tom Bellini is not on this short list, though. Hallie's opinion of him, voiced at the slightest opportunity, is that he's not a serious person. His faithlessness, which began in the first year of his and Jesse's marriage, along with his hypochondria and self-dramatizing and petulance in the face of disappointment, were all signs, she says, of a pampered childhood.

"Let his family have him back," she said when he left Jesse and the kids and the swim school and Venus Beach in a peel of rubber out the driveway. "They deserve him."

Whenever his name comes up, as it does now, Hallie is poised to go after him. Jesse puts up a hand to stop this. "He's not even down here yet. I don't want to have to think about him one second sooner than I have to. Tell me about the boyfriend."

Hallie lets go of her security knob and starts going through her oversize handbag, so stuffed its clasp is permanently wedged open. She pulls out a fat yellow package, plucks a snapshot off the top of the stack, and hands it over to Jesse. Who pulls off to the side of the road and props it against the coat-of-arms center of the Hog's steering wheel so she can get a good look.

The guy in the picture, who appears to be about a decade younger than her mother (around whose shoulders his arm is draped) is wearing a black shirt and slacks with a white belt and boots. His hair is the too black of home dye jobs, maybe Grecian Formula.

"He's in rock and roll," Hallie says. "He plays pedal steel in this rowdy group that headlines over at the Blue Light on weekends. B. Sting."

Jesse looks at Darrell again and tries to figure how he and her mother link up, from what oblique angles they can possibly approach each other.

"You think he's after her money?" Jesse says to Hallie.

"That king's ransom in savings bonds and pass book accounts? Please. If anything, he's giving up more than she is. He has a house back up in some holler, down in Arkansas, but he's thinking of moving into town to be with her."

"This sounds serious."

"Wellll, let's just say I wouldn't be surprised to hear wedding bells ringing sometime soon."

"Oh, Hallie," Jesse says breathlessly, putting her hand on her godmother's pantsuited knee, then shifting into drive as she gets back on the highway, "they don't *have* to get married, do they?"

After picking up Hallie's dog, Sweetie, at the kennel, they go to Hallie's apartment, where, once Jesse has brought in the luggage, and Hallie has rolled up the hurricane shutters and opened all the windows to get a cross breeze going and put on a pot of Mr. Coffee — an all-day beverage where she and Jesse come from — they sit down side by side on the sofa bed and go through the rest of the photos, most of which are from the party.

A ways into them, Jesse says, "Now I'm kind of sorry I didn't come up," then notices who's missing. "Hey. Where's the Cowboy? Why wasn't Willie there?"

"Oh, they switched his shift on him at the last minute, and you know he absolutely won't miss work." For almost a year now, William has had a job at the McDonald's out-side New Jerusalem. "It really suits him," Hallie says. "He packs all the Happy Meal boxes and keeps all the napkins and straws and ketchup packet bins refilled, and empties the trash and polices the lot. He's really good. And I don't just mean good for a retarded person. He was Employee of the Month."

"I know. He called from Mama's. He was so excited."

"They put his name on the special parking space."

"But he doesn't drive."

"Well, so what?" Hallie says, as though Jesse is the one acting retarded. "The whole group home thing has been good for him, and there's you to thank for that."

Jesse went up to help her mother with this a couple of years back, to cut through all the red tape. Frances just couldn't have done it by herself, even though everyone agreed it was time Willie got out on his own more, got used to living without his mother in anticipation of a time when he might have to.

"It would just make you so pleased, I'm sure," Hallie says. "The house staff — Lois and Dan, you remember him — make sure the residents don't get too far off track. But basically they fend for themselves, and it seems to make them go further than you'd expect. I went over for dinner once, and for a patch of time, you'd think you were just at the dinner table of a regular family." She catches Jesse's look and scales down. "Well, an *ir*-regular family."

Hallie has also brought some mail, passed along by Jesse's mother. She dumps the rubber-banded packet onto Jesse's lap. "I'm not sure what all there is."

The first piece of interest is a booklet from Jesse's twen-tieth high school reunion, which she missed.

"Oh, you would've been the star of that," Hallie says as Jesse flips through, looking at the "then and now" pictures. "Wow. What happened to Louise Franz?"

Hallie pushes her reading glasses down her nose, and peers over the top of the frames. "They say she drinks a bit."

"Boy. She looks like a marshmallow. She used to be so cute. So perky. Wow, here's Laurel."

"She's back in town," Hallie says. "Her husband has work nearby. I ran into her at the beauty shop. She asked after you, of course. I souped you up a bit."

"How? That line about me being the aquatic director of The Academy?"

"Well that, of course. And then it just came to me to say you'd won the Pillsbury Bake-Off."

"Hallie!" Jesse says when she sees it's not a joke, and starts laughing. "What did I make?"

"A tamale pie."

"Oh my."

Jesse is on to the letters, mostly the odd request to speak before local groups of young people on "The Making of a Champion" or "The Will to Win."

"No one was ever prouder of anyone than I was of you that day," Hallie says, launching into a subject she knows Jesse doesn't like rumpled, but Hallie can't help herself. "Seeing you win."

"But I didn't."

"You got a medal. I don't believe they give medals to losers. Oh, and some girl called you from there," Hallie says. "Another swimmer." She rummages through her over-stuffed purse and pulls out an equally overstuffed peach leatherette wallet bursting with cleaners' receipts and supermarket tapes and phone numbers of clients. Sweetie pokes her nose in and sniffs these. "Now, where did I put that slip?"

"Maybe this is it," Jesse says, snatching at a promising scrap. She reads it, then hands it back to Hallie. All it says is "cinnamon floss."

Hallie checks it out. "Oh. Renee, my hygienist, says it's terrific; I've been meaning to get some." Hallie goes back to her rooting and almost immediately comes up with the right one. "Here's your friend." She hands it to Jesse.

"Evelyn Spencer," Jesse reads aloud. She can hear her voice, flattened like a movie mummy fresh from the crypt.

Hallie, who prides herself in not missing much, says, "Perhaps we were expecting someone else?"

Friday afternoon, Jesse is teaching her Scared to Death class. She has six students. Breathing is the biggest part of their problem. If she could just pass a little tray of cocktails around before class. As it is, she has to mellow the students out herself, the hard way — distracting them from their worst fears, which are all really the exact same fear. She has worked out a little program combining some poolside yoga, some New Age tapes, and a "go for it" atmosphere. When this all comes together, it works pretty well. Today, however, is not a high point.

Jesse's favorite student, Dolores Huerta, a Cuban woman who is acutely hydrophobic, but very plucky and determined, has just taken in a large amount of water through her nose. She is gagging and coughing and alternately pointing at herself and flapping her thin arms around like a crazed, rickety penguin. As the five other students look on, faces bleached with terror, Jesse reaches an arm across Dolores's bony chest and, with the other hand, chops her several times between the shoulder blades.

It's at this moment that Tom Bellini comes through the archway to the pool, into Jesse's life for the first time in three years. Sharon, who Jesse knows has been waiting for his car all afternoon, comes out of the house and goes all gawky when her dad hugs her, dropping her shoulders like a marionette. She takes him into the house while Jesse hauls Dolores out of the drink and onto a chaise where she continues to cough wet little coughs. Jesse hops back in the water and tells the others, "Hey! No problem!"

They stand and look at her with wild eyes, pupils dilated. They spend the rest of the hour just getting through it. When they've all gone, probably never to return, Jesse dries off, pulls on shorts and a T-shirt over her bathing suit, and goes inside.

Sharon has set out a little spread that tears Jesse's heart in its desire to please. Sardines on crackers and little ham salad triangle sandwiches with the crusts cut off. She and Tom are having glasses of Perrier with lime. Jesse acts extremely casual around this. She can tell she is supposed to pretend they do this every afternoon — pause genteelly, a little teatimey tradition. She also notices there's an old, but freshly pressed cloth on the contact-papered kitchen table. And that the recliner has been pulled out of the kitchen, into a corner of the living room, its missing arm obscured against the wall, camouflaged under an avalanche of throw pillows.

Tom is sitting on a lawn chair, his legs crossed at the knees. He's wearing creamy linen pants and a washed silk shirt. The gentleman caller.

"Your drowning class?" He nods out toward the pool as she comes into the room.

Just as Jesse is thinking that, except for a haircut that is long and locky in the back, he looks much the same, he says, "Boy, Jess. You're getting to look more and more like your mother."

This isn't good. Her mother looks like someone painted by Grant Wood. Jesse reaches up with both hands and rumples her wet hair. As if this is going to make a big difference. As if messing up her hair is going to transform her from a six-foot rangy redhead approaching middle age with an old crick acting up in her back and a wet swimsuit soaking through her shorts, into someone hot. Into Cher.

"The old place looks great," Tom says now, easing into a deep soak of nostalgia. Transforming Jesse's hard present into a heart-tugging past. In his version, the school isn't a dilapidated anachronism; it's the definition of old-fashioned charm. She hates this. He knows better. She can still see him in his last years here, after he'd figured out that the fame of an Olympic athlete is only slightly longer than everyone's allotted fifteen minutes. After he'd discovered that the pipes underneath the Bud Barris Academy were in worse repair than its portals. After he'd seen that in hard times — of which there were many seasons in Venus Beach — the first thing people drop is their kids' swim lessons.

This was where he began to lose interest. Tom saw life as an adventure, an endearing quality in the short run, but one which left him uninterested in dealing with the largish parts of life which turned out to be less than adventures. And so while he could be counted on to take the kids to Safari Land and the Serpentarium, he never once sat in the waiting room of the pediatrician's office. As a family unit, they functioned more like a mother, her two kids, and their swinging bachelor uncle.

Jesse can pull up a perfect picture of Tom near the end, sitting in the back office, eyebrows bunched together, eyes pouchy from so many hours sitting between the mint-colored canvas-back ledger and the old, crank-operated adding machine, trying to make the red numbers do gymnastics, hurtle into the black, trying to put the fun back into things. When he couldn't, he left. But that's a sad memory, so he tints the fatigued truth with sepia.

Jesse leaps in with wild lies, to defend her life from his appreciation. "We're going to put in a diving pool out back. We're to the point where we've got to expand, or burst at the seams. Some guy came by last month and wanted to franchise us in five southern markets."

These days Tom is back in New York, working for his father. Over the years, BelliniSport has become a minor contender in the sportswear trade. When Jesse met him, though, it was still Bellini Brothers, a sweatshop in Newark, which cranked out racing suits and flocked team T-shirts. His father, Rocco, had higher aspirations and sent Tom down to Mexico City, to the Olympics, to try to pick up endorsements from medalists for a line of women's racing suits. Jesse was ambivalent, shy.

That fall, he came to see her again in Missouri. He had a mock-up of the suit with him — blue with maroon and white trim.

It was on the ten-city promotion tour for this suit, in a room in the Drake Hotel in Chicago, that Jesse went to bed with Tom. They were both extremely inexperienced, and so the event took on greater significance than it might have otherwise. They felt linked by it and began hatching their ideas for Tom to escape his family's business, for Jesse to flee New Jerusalem and the dead sure sequence of life events that awaited her there.

Now Tom has remarried, is on to a new adventure. Jesse was sure he would find some model a couple of decades younger than he is. Instead, and worse in a hard-to-explain way, he married a woman a little older than Jesse, the Bellini account exec at their ad agency. Jesse hates each of the very few things she knows about Kyra. The first is that Kyra is her entire name.

"Oh, get real. What's her last name?" she asked Tom.

"I think that's Kyra's business," he told her.

Kyra wears only black. It's her signature color. Jesse tries to imagine all the things that would have to be different about her own life in order for her to have a signature color.

"Kyra says why don't you come up for a couple of weeks during your vacation," Tom is telling Sharon now. "You haven't seen the bambinos yet."

Jesse hasn't seen the bambinos, hasn't even met Kyra. She wasn't invited to the wedding. Sharon was, and she came back with the report that Kyra was "kind of neat." She's forty-one to Tom's forty-four. Time was pressing in on them, so right off, they had her last-chance baby, which turned out to be the twins.

"Some pics of the rug rats," he's saying now, passing them around. When he takes the snapshots back, he looks through them and restrains himself (but not quite hard enough) from smiling. Then slides them back into his wallet.

"So," he says, drinking down his Perrier as he stands up into his man of action mode, as though everyone else is reclining on chaises, fanning themselves. "I'd better get moving on this. Hustle my butt down to Delray and talk to Handelman. It would be great if we could just lay a little incentive on the guy who owns the BMW." His blowfish routine, puffing himself up to deal with scarier forms of life in the tank.

When they are outside in the parking lot, standing around his rented Olds, black with tinted windows, he says, "On my way back I thought I'd pick up Anthony. And what's-her-name."

"Lynette," Sharon says.

"The Eskimo," Jesse says.

"I thought we could all go out for dinner."

When he's at the end of the drive, turning onto the county road, Jesse says to Sharon, "Can't I be washing my hair?"

"Come on," says Sharon, who just wants everything to be all right. "It's just one dinner. We'll all be together again. It'll be nice. You'll see."

"Oh, honey."

The phone rings just as Jesse is coming out of the shower.

"Sharon!" she calls out, but the phone keeps ringing. She knows Sharon isn't answering so she won't have to go through the disappointment of it not being Ian. She blots the water off her hair with a stiff towel while she rushes down the short hall and into her bedroom and picks up.

It's Oscar. "I just got this thing installed. The guy just left. Now I can grill steaks right on the stove, without ever leaving my realm of air-conditioned splendor. My life is now totally perfect, complete. And I want you to share it with me."

"The steak," Jesse says.

"Yes," Oscar says. "Look, I know it's short notice — "

"And I'd love to, you know it, but this is happy family night. A heartwarming dinner at the Cattleman's. I'm sorry you won't be there to share this joy of the moment with us."

Oscar doesn't say anything. She can hear the soft, whippy sound of pages being turned, and knows he is skimming the instruction booklet that came with the grill. She tries to make him feel bad for caring so little about her small sorrows.

"Oscar, I'm just dragged down with too much family at the moment. I'll be fun again soon, I promise."

"I'll keep the massage oil on warm," he says. Oscar is extremely deft at ducking an argument.

The Cattleman's Corral has a huge parking lot marked off by a ranch fence. Jesse and Sharon pull in next to Tom's rental car and get out of the Hog and start toward the restaurant, both of them awkward in heels. There's a flapping sound at their backs. Sharon doesn't even have to turn around. "No problem with *those* wipers," she says to Jesse.

The restaurant is Lynette's choice. "They have an endless salad bar," she told Jesse on the phone.

"The Beef Baron sounds good," Anthony says, looking at the menu.

"We guarantee thirty-two ounces of meat," says the waitress in a voice dulled by having had to say this too many million times. "It's for your heartier appetite."

"They put you in a deep pit, then throw the meat in after you," Sharon says.

"I'll try it," says Anthony.

Sharon, who has ordered fried shrimp every single time Jesse has ever been in a restaurant with her, going back to when she still said "schwimp," finishes intently studying her menu, looks up, and says, "I think I'll have the fried shrimp."

The waitress turns to Jesse, who says, "I'm having trouble deciding between the fish *du jour* and the catch of the day." Then immediately feels crummy for fooling around while this woman, who has had to serve too many giant hunks of meat and defrosted filets of fish, has to wait for her. "What do you recommend?" she says, trying to get serious.

"I like the Neptune's Platter," the waitress says, and her voice lifts a little into the realm of the living, so Jesse knows it's not a formula response.

"Then that's what I'll have." Actually, tonight Jesse would just as soon skip the food component of this meal entirely, and order an IV with a Valium drip.

Tom, she can tell, is enjoying his small moment, at the head of the table, as it were, although the table is actually round. Basking in good feeling and fond memories. It's like he's here on a package tour of his past. The kids like seeing him, it's clear. Jesse still worries that in the middle of their darker nights, they hate her for not being able to love their father.

Everyone takes a long time at the salad bar, which features, along with the usual torn lettuce and tomato wedges and chickpeas and bacon bits, a table with hot trays of chicken wings and corned beef and cabbage and macaroni and cheese and red Jell-O and bread pudding. Back at the table, their dinners are waiting. At Jesse's place is a plate filled with a variety of small, batter-covered objects.

"Good shrimp," Sharon says. Even as she's sitting down, she's already pulling a tail out of her mouth.

Tom pours white wine for himself and Jesse out of a

heavy amber carafe. He wanted to order a bottle, but they have it only by the glass, or in carafes tapped from the cardboard boxes at the end of the bar.

Anthony and Lynette watch as the waitress sets their Cokes down in front of them. They're shy in this social situation. They've dressed up. Lynette has on a skirt of something vaguely snakeskinny. She has the white, chick-fluff hair of the girls pictured in *People* heading into trendy clubs on the arms of heavy metal stars. It's as though she's picking up night signals from some heated social center, all the way out here in this remote locale where none of what she's ready for is happening.

Anthony looks the part of her boyfriend. He has an ankh symbol dangling from one ear, is wearing a muscle T-shirt to expose his tattoo. Jesse tries, not very successfully, not to let this tattoo upset her. The picture is four claws tearing their way out through the skin from inside.

Although they look like they're on leave from a coven, Anthony and Lynette act like they're going steady. They kiss long, soft kisses, then stare into each other's eyes for minutes on end while the conversation pauses as everyone else gives in to their involuntary fascination with them.

Lynette whispers to him a lot. At first Jesse thinks this is about real secrets and then notices that, for instance, Lynette will whisper to Anthony and he'll nod and then pass her the salt. She cuts his meat for him, which is not so terrible as it might be. It is, after all, the Beef Baron, and he does, after all, have a bandaged hand.

It's not easy to draw them into the table talk. Tom tries. He's a P.R. guy, adept at entry-level chat. "So Lynette," he says, swelling his voice, "I hear you have some pretty in-teresting dogs."

She nods through a mouthful of sunflower seeds. Although it was the endless salad bar she recommended here, her own salad ends quite abruptly. It is ninety-nine percent sunflower seeds on about three pieces of lettuce. Finally, the crunching stops and she says, "We're teaching them to talk."

No one thinks of anything to say to this.

A band is setting up, five guys, a wide range of ages and styles. All of them are in white dinner jackets gone yellow at the seams. According to their drum, they're the Rhythmaires. *Taptaptap* goes the trumpet player, an index finger thudding deafeningly on the microphone, followed by a feisty screech of amp backlash.

"Oh boy," Jesse says.

"It'll be funny," Sharon says.

"We are the Rhythmaires," says the trumpet player. "Specializing in pop, show tunes, country favorites, polkas, rock and roll, and lambada!"

Anthony holds his head as though all his wisdom teeth have impacted.

Sharon looks across the table at him and crosses her eyes. She takes Lynette's hand and pulls her out onto the floor. Jesse knows Sharon doesn't really like Lynette much, but is trying like crazy, for Anthony's sake. As far as Jesse can tell, in the world lineup of goodness, there's Mother Teresa, then there's Sharon. When William came to visit in the spring, Sharon let him style her hair with the blow dryer nearly every morning (he is preoccupied with this lately; it has to do with a crush he has on the girl who cuts his hair in New Jerusalem), and went to school looking whatever way she did.

*

When Sharon and Anthony and Lynette are all out on the dance floor, fooling around to "New York, New York," annoying the few old couples on the floor, who still take their fox trotting seriously, it occurs to Jesse that the kids — Anthony and Lynette, not Sharon — are probably high.

Tom and Jesse watch from the table. He orders the two of them brandies, which come in snifters nearly the size and thickness of dime store fishbowls.

"He's a good kid," Tom says, nodding toward the dance floor. As if saying this will make it so. "What is all this, really? A little trouble. A speck. It's the sort of thing boys get into." Jesse tunes out while he explains boys to her.

"Maybe you could take him up north," she says. "Get him something at Bellini. Stockroom or something. I'd like to see him Say No to Lynette. I think she's the French Connection."

"Ah," Tom says. He nods, as if slowly contemplating the wisdom of this suggestion. Jesse can see him synchromeshing through the gears to get to the reason he won't be able to do this. Although he'd love to, of course.

"I'd love to, of course," he says. "But I'm an old guy for parenthood, for babies. They get one virus after another and then Kyra's down with it and then I am. I don't think I can do babies *and* Anthony, if you know what I mean."

Jesse drifts off and watches Anthony dancing with Lynette. It's a slow number, "Moon River," and they're basically standing still in the center of the floor, just swaying slightly from side to side. Sharon is dancing with some guy in his thirties, who's been sitting at the bar. He's got on an overly colorful sweatshirt that makes him look like he's just won the Grand Prix. He's big, and he's hulking over Sharon in a sexy way Jesse doesn't like. Lighten up, she tells herself, and turns back to Tom.

He lets his hand catch his head and prop it close to her face. He's about to get serious, she can tell. She tries to head him off with gossip. "My mother's got herself a boyfriend."

He nods as if he's absorbing this information, then says, "You should consider it yourself, Jess. Really. You're still young."

Although about ninety percent of what Tom says makes Jesse go ballistic inside, she keeps a cool surface. Does he really think she leads a life of swim lessons and celibacy? He knows Oscar. It's a small town. Tom and Jesse bought the last car of their marriage from him, the car Tom later drove north into his new life. What Tom doesn't know about is Oscar and Jesse. She doesn't bother telling him; she couldn't score any points with it. He would just see it as one more indication of her being charmingly rooted forever in this sleepy backwater he himself has left behind.

"Guess who I ran into at the sportswear show?" he says after a while of staring out at the dance floor.

"Buffalo Bob."

"Marty Finch."

Jesse has had a bit too much wine and brandy to gather up all the cords of control she would like to have. She can only hope she's doing a passable impersonation of someone whose heart is not slamming around inside her chest like a tuna.

"Oh."

"We had this All-Time Greats banquet. I sent you an invite, remember? Brought in some big names. Schollander. Shane Gould. Spitz was supposed to show, but he didn't. Anyway, good old Marty was there."

Jesse tries to think of a question that would seem reasonable. "How did she seem?"

"Oh, full of it. She's a trip. Still looks like a photo neg-
ative. You know, that platinum hair and Coppertone tan.
She's got a TV show down there. Not like the underwater
detective thing. A talk show. Interviews celebrities."

A couple of hundred questions leap instantly to mind.
Jesse carefully picks the top one off the deck. "Did she ask
after me?"

"It was a real crowd," Tom says. "I only got to talk with
her for a few minutes. You know." He swooshes what's left
of his brandy around so it's only a lining on the inside of the
glass. "Do you ever think about it anymore?" he says.
"Your big moment?"

Jesse tries to tell if he's being sarcastic, capitalizing *Big*
and *Moment,* but she decides he probably isn't, that he
sincerely wants to know. And it's an okay question, really.
People ask it from time to time. But still.

She shakes her head "no." So often she finds lying just
has the right feel to it.

Tom sleeps in Anthony's bedroom and picks up after himself when he showers and shaves, something he never did
when he lived here. He's a model guest in the conventional
ways. But he is intent on making his presence count, on
getting everybody agitated. He leaves every morning, usually with Sharon in tow, to pick up Anthony and go cruising
the intracoastal in a Sea Skiff belonging to an old friend
from his days down here. Or he takes them to one of the
pricier malls to shop for clothes. At night, they hit the dog
track or jai alai.

"A few quality days with my kids is all I want," he tells
Jesse, who is invited along on these excursions, but the
invitation is always cast in such a way that it's clear demur-
ring is the expected response.

The day before Anthony's hearing, Jesse insists on coming along. Tom has been counting on settling out of court, but Handelman, the turbo lawyer, isn't able to buy off the guy with the BMW, whose stereo was the third that had been ripped out of one or another of his dashboards. This guy, with whom they have a fifteen-minute meeting, is much closer to being Bernie Goetz than being the kind of guy who would give Anthony a pass. Handelman *does* get a continuance, but Anthony is going to have to go to court soon, and then probably to the work farm for a while.

"Still," Tom tells them all as they drive back in the frigid air conditioning of the rental car, "I think things are going to work out just fine in the long run." He says this with the assurance of a character in the final moments of a TV drama, putting a tidy resolution on the preceding hour. To celebrate the conclusion of this episode, he reaches back through the space between the front seats to give Anthony a high five slap. Mr. Good Dad.

"Meanwhile, back in the real world . . . " Jesse says, to no one in particular.

The next morning, when Tom's packing to leave, folding his shirts with an amazing precision, a talent gained through years on the road of sales, he tells Jesse, "Anthony's going to be all right. He's beyond the drug thing now, he told me. It was just an experimenting phase. Lynette's helping him. She's a good kid, too. Don't worry so much about everything." Jesse knows this isn't all. She distinctly feels a pronouncement poised in the air between them, but doesn't move fast enough to duck it. "You know my philosophy," Tom tells her. "Just give them too much love."

She looks at him, haloed in the light coming through the open window, and regrets for the first time that this is a one-story house.

In the next few weeks it becomes clear that something is wrong with Anthony's hand; a nerve was lacerated and isn't really coming back. The surgeon recommends physical therapy, and Jesse begins to take Anthony three afternoons a week over to a place called SportsMed. He doesn't have wheels anymore. When Lynette took a hard look at Anthony's current situation, she decided he wasn't going to be any fun at all, and took off, with the station wagon and the dogs.

Although he still speaks to her only in portion-controlled syllables, Jesse allows herself to think something better is beginning to happen between them. And then she thinks she's kidding herself.

And then the storms come on, almost always at night, nearly a week's worth of them. Either she can't sleep on account of rumbling in the distance, a feeling of something looming at the edge of her consciousness. Or she can just get to sleep, barely, and then is pulled from it by a sharp crack of lightning, or by nocturnal events that come along with the storms, that begin to seem like part of the agitated weather, that start making it seem as though the nights are a pulsing underneath the smooth, flat surface of the days.

The first night event slides into the middle of a dream Jesse is having that's like a murder mystery. It's raining outside. There's a bloody body on her floor. She's not responsible, but knows no one will believe her. The doorbell rings. She doesn't know whether to answer.

As she awakens, she begins to understand it's not the

doorbell, but the phone. She lies still, listening to it ring against the backdrop of a hard rain falling outside, dunning the flat roof above her. She wonders where the nightmare came from, then remembers the soap opera she was half watching in the SportsMed waiting lounge. A nurse murdering her contemptuous doctor lover. A nurse with a bad hand, like Anthony.

She lets the machine pick up. In the middle of the night, she has found this is best. It's usually a heavy breather, or someone at a pay phone in an extremely loud bar looking for Audrey, who seems to have an active social life and a phone number a digit over from Jesse's.

But this time it's Hallie, sounding awful. Jesse reaches over and picks up, breaking in. "What?" Jesse says. "What's wrong?"

"I don't know. Something I ate, maybe. Muriel talked me into going to this Chinese place." Hallie is suspicious of all ethnic cuisines, but particularly Chinese. She is certain they use cat meat. "Maybe it's my appendix, but I think they took that out when they did the hysterectomy."

"I'll be right up," Jesse says.

"Not in this rain."

"It's okay," Jesse says. Hallie never asks for anything. She pulls on the jeans and cutoff sweatshirt puddled next to the bed.

"What's happening?" Sharon asks, tottering in, fresh from sleep and still off balance. She looks like she's tripping along on little pig hooves. "Was it Ian?"

"Hallie. She's sick. I'll go up there."

"Okay," she says, not having really woken up. She crumples onto Jesse's bed and is asleep before she hits the mattress.

*

The rain is a sort Jesse never saw before she came to Florida, a solid wall of water. She can almost feel its pressure against the windshield; it's like going through a car wash. The few other cars ahead of her are just blurry red lights. She can't go over ten miles per hour, both because she can't see, and because the drainless streets are awash, water whipping across them, forming great rushing gulleys in low spots.

Finally — it takes her almost an hour instead of the usual twenty minutes — she gets to Hallie's. She makes a mad dash across the lawn and starts to grope under her poncho for her key, but Hallie is already on the other side, opening the door. Her color looks gray against the blue plushy robe she's wearing. Sweetie roams nervously around her legs.

"You poor, drowned rat. And now I feel silly yanking you all the way up here. I feel quite a bit better since I threw up."

"No, I'm dry as toast under here," Jesse says, pulling off the poncho, shaking it out on the porch, then hanging it on a doorknob. She leaves her sandals in the hallway, then follows Hallie in. "Besides, you saved me from myself. I was dreaming I was a murderer."

"Funny. When I woke up with this, I was dreaming you were married to Liberace. I hated your furniture, but I didn't want to tell you."

Jesse sits down next to her on the folded-out sofa bed, then pats the sheets beneath them, which are soaked with night sweat. Hallie suddenly goes quiet and looks much worse.

"If you'll excuse me for a moment," she says with Missouri politeness. She goes into the bathroom and is there quite a while. When she comes out, Jesse is remaking the bed with fresh sheets. She helps Hallie sit down in her recliner and asks, "Do you think we should go to the hospital?"

"No, I'm much better now. I think the worst is over."

Jesse looks at her skeptically.

"Really."

"Stay there a minute," Jesse says, running a hand through Hallie's damp hair. Then goes into the bathroom and begins running a tub.

"I'm just a little wobbly," she says as Jesse lowers her into the warm water, then washes her with a cloth and soap that smells like berries.

"I brought some chamomile," Jesse says. "I'll go fix you some. You stay in here a little while. Relax. You want company?"

"Yes. Come back soon." Jesse thinks this may be the first time she has ever seen Hallie frightened.

When she brings the tea, she sets a cup on the edge of the bath, puts the lid down on the toilet, making it her chair. She pulls her knees up to her chest.

Hallie looks over at the tea as though she is being persecuted with having to drink it.

"It's herbal," Jesse says. "Elaine put me on to it."

"I know about herbal. I knew about herbal before it was cool. *Way* before," Hallie says. "It's icky," she says after a sip, making her mouth into a prune.

"Nope. Good — and good *for* you."

After quite some while of Hallie looking at her in a peculiar — intent yet distant — way, Jesse asks, "What are you thinking?"

"Oh. This is from so far back. When you were a girl. I

stopped by one afternoon on the way home from the parlor, knocked on your mother's back door, and got no answer. I figured she was downstairs with the washer running and couldn't hear me. But when I got inside I could hear you squalling. And then I heard a slap, and then dead silence. I came into the living room. I didn't have to see, but at the same time I did. And then you saw me. You were sitting on the sofa with a little red face and a hardness in your eyes."

"What did you do?"

"Oh, not much of anything really. People hit their kids, I know that. And I'm sure your mother never did it to you but once or twice."

"I don't even remember the once," Jesse says.

"There you go. And who knows, maybe you deserved it. You've always had a smart mouth on you. You probably want to hear that I told her if she ever struck you again, I'd stand witness to it on Judgment Day. But this was the fifties. And New Jerusalem, as you know, is not a place where things happen in a big, dramatic way. Not like in *our* city." By which she means Rome.

"And I didn't really have to say anything. It was enough — too much almost — that I was even standing there, enough that she saw censure in my eyes. Our friendship foundered for a time after that. It was only after a while that she let me back into her good graces, only after I'd gone through a time of being punished. I'd violated convention, you see. No matter how much I loved you, my proper place was outside, on the other side of that screen door, politely knocking, then waiting until I was allowed in. And except for that one time, I've always kept to my place — outside, at arm's length, at a respectable distance.

And all it has gotten me in the end is that I'm alone. And I don't like it."

"But alone is how you've chosen to live your whole life."

"Well, not really," Hallie says.

"You didn't choose it?"

"I wasn't quite alone," she says, dropping as if it were a feather, an anvil. Having gotten confessional, Hallie seems to be on a roll.

"Oh my," Jesse says, and feels herself starting to blush. "Well, I guess I always knew. I just never knew *who*."

"Oh, don't go wide-eyed on me. You look like a vulture. It's not exactly fascinating information anyway. It was only Horace."

At first Jesse doesn't get who's being talked about. Then suddenly she does. "Doc Wemby?!"

"He was a fine man," Hallie says defensively. "And a great physician."

"Well, I know that," Jesse says, backpeddling. "I'm sorry. I'm laughing at myself, for being such a jerk. It's like I can't imagine the generation older than me in love. How teenage."

"No. You just can't imagine a secret life would be necessary to loving a round, jolly man with a bad toupee and a Say Ahh sampler on his office wall. But really, who'd you think it was going to be, Ricardo Montalban?"

Jesse can't think of a good comeback, and so just gives over to babbling. "But, I mean, those four kids? I mean five, counting Keith." And then she slaps her head, catching herself just too late to stop this cartoon gesture. "My sponsor! The poor guy. He probably didn't give a fig about swimming!

"Doc Wemby," she says again a few moments later, still

tapering off in her amazement as she gets Hallie out of the tub and blots her dry with a big towel, then puts Sarah Vaughan low on the stereo, and brings Hallie out onto her little patio. The rain has stopped as suddenly as it started; everything is dripping and smelling of reawakening.

The next night event starts so late it barely comes in under the wire of dawn. Jesse has been sleeping restlessly, first through hard cracks of thunder, photoflash lightning bursts, and then a short while of pelting rain. It doesn't even feel as though she's been sleeping, except that she wakes to the sound of distant splashing that wasn't there before. Sometimes neighborhood dogs get in. One time she found a small alligator in the shallow end. It pays to take a look.

She pulls on shorts and a shirt, picks up a bread knife from the kitchen counter, and pads barefoot through the breezeway. When she gets to the pool door, she stops and looks out between the open jalousie louvers. There are boys, one, two . . . four of them. It takes a while for her to see through the shadows that one of them is Anthony.

The others she doesn't recognize. Anthony's friends are always strangers to her, and never seem to be around long enough to become familiar. From the goofy way they're talking to each other, the laughter that comes too easily from jokes too dumb, she guesses they are stoned. They've turned on the underwater lights and have shed their clothes and are variously diving and falling into the water, then barreling up to the surface, breaking through shouting, shaking the water from their whipping fans of long hair, spraying it from their mouths, their pale skin blue, as they emerge into the moonlight, washed clear by the storm.

Soon they grow tired and fall onto the gym mats at the far end of the pool. Only Anthony remains standing; he's on the lip of the pool for so long and in such a state of perfect suspension, he looks like a failed statue, too frail to be made of stone. And then in one fluid move, he is in the air, out over the water, then onto it and taking the length of the pool with a machinery of strokes, getting rid of the water standing in his way.

Jesse knows he knows she's watching. And that he's showing her, not what he can do, but what he won't.

These stormy nights leave behind a sky the blue of Hawaiian shirts, prom dresses, the inside of Woolworth jewelry boxes. Jesse cruises into town, picking up some coffee at the doughnut shop, then heads up A1A to a short stretch of tourist-free beach she uses as a thinking spot. There are PRIVATE—KEEP OFF signs, but she has never run into anyone enforcing them.

She cuts a fast right off the highway onto the sand and stops just shy of the breakers. She snaps an old Stones tape into Sharon's Walkman, pushes the tiny speakers into her ears, and gets out and boosts herself up onto the hood. She needs to retreat for a while, from the present.

Usually, if she looks at the ocean long enough, then closes her eyes, the color will come up. The part she can't control is where the scene will open. Sometimes it's the dead white, and she is down in the showers, Marty's breath on her, hot; the night air cool, clinging to the tiles. And the dogs, something about their yelping exciting her, making her think of search parties, translating this into fear of discovery. Discovery of what, though?

This time the frame that comes up is an earlier one, the

color is still aquamarine, the pool bottom as she streaks over it. When she turns her head to the side to breathe, she can see she has only a quarter of the pool length left to go. She can also see that Marty is ever so slightly behind her. And then Jesse can feel herself, just the slightest bit, slowing down her stroke, spreading her fingers in the water to let the blue-green flow between them, relinquishing purchase. All of this so that her hand, when it slaps the tile at the end, will do so the smallest increment of measurable time after Marty's. Taking the biggest moment of her life and blowing it off. For love. Making a spectacular gesture Marty would never know about, and if she did, would probably feel more contempt for than appreciation. The definition of folly.

Jesse can't be sure about this, of course. She can't tell if she is really remembering this, if this is the way it actually happened. Or if it is simply a device of self-torture, pulling the drape off the unthinkable thought.

She stares out at the sun, which has just lifted itself off the horizon, tastes the salt on her thumb as she drags it across her lower lip. Inside her earphones, she's backed by "Tumbling Dice." "My my my," Mick Jagger slides into her ears, "I'm the lone crapshooter."

She is sitting on the rust-pocked hood of a way too old car as she looks out on a dying sea. She's pushing forty, with a failing business, two Visas maxed to the gills, a truly stupid marriage behind her, two kids already cruising into their own disappointed adulthoods. What can this pitiful bubble of history mean to her now that it has been paved over by so much real life?

She has never been able to tell anyone that this nonsense still tumbles around inside her. She worries it indicates an essential foolishness, and that maybe this is where Anthony comes by his. She would like to save him from this legacy, but her dreams of salvation are too unfocused. She can't see what shore she could bring him to. Still, she'd like to be able to toss the rope within his reach and feel the tug of his grabbing on.

She should pry herself away from here, light out for the territory, wherever that might be. Sometimes, particularly on windless days like this one, she thinks she might truly die with longing for something to get her out of here, something to at least point her in some direction. Instead she sits here on the hood of her car, or lies on the sofa late at night, watching TV for clues. The modern dramas bleed, as the night wears on, into dated ones with cigarette holders and veiled hats, but all of them are about lives lived breathlessly, on heights with a steep dropoff. She has a brief acquaintance with this geography herself, but getting worked up about it does no good at all. Just leaves her sitting here all turned around, looking forward to the past.

Sandgate

JESSE HAS BEEN SITTING in a room in the Travelodge
for two days, passing up the Koala Sanctuary and the Dev-
onshire Tea Cruise recommended by the front desk clerk,
who couldn't know she is a traveler of a different sort, a
tourist in her own past.

She hasn't told anyone about coming down here. Smoke
in their eyes, a light dusting of deceit, so they won't be able
to see her for the little while she needs to disappear.

All she has is an address, in a beach town up the coast a
bit. Sandgate. A resort town of another era. This from the
Olympic alum newsletter. ("Marty Finch asks her old pals,
one and all, to write.")

What she has done for these two days is sleep and gather
up her momentum and watch TV, sifting through Lucy
reruns and numbingly educational programs on wildlife
and ancient civilizations and the nervous system. Finally
she finds Marty's show, "Q & A," which appears to be a
deadly earnest interview-format half hour.

"How did you see yourself and Parallelogram breaking away from what you call the 'grounding' of earlier dance movements?" Marty leans in, posing an intent question to an extremely thin, middle-aged man in a black turtleneck coiled in the chair opposite her.

She looks — not the same, of course not. Not at all, really. She's so much older, in the middle of her adulthood instead of where Jesse left her, at its beginning. But the differences between Marty's then self and this one — her mouth and eyes now set within fine lines, the tan which has lost its freshness — are irrelevant in the face of the sameness of everything significant. Jesse knows, just from what she can see on this snowy motel TV screen, that Marty is, in everything essential, the same.

Jesse throws the shift into overdrive and feels the engine of the rented Fourunner kick in as she passes a cluster of poky cars and delivery vans. Idly, she wonders if there's a speed limit in Australia. She pulls over onto the gravel shoulder and checks the road atlas spread out on the passenger seat, anchored by a chocolate doughnut. She picks up a smaller, pencil-drawn map the guy at the gas station a few miles back made for her. She sees she has missed the turnoff and has to double-back two mile markers. From there, though, it's a breeze, and in a few minutes she is near the sea, can smell it before she sees it, can see the high-flying water birds — sea eagles and kingfishers — swooping down, soaring up again. And then she is coming up on the house described by the gas station guy. It's the last in a small line of old holiday houses, across the road from the beach, set up on stilts covered with latticework to let the breeze through, a Colonial conceit in gentle decline, battered by hard winds of other, less clement days, its wooden veranda sagging a bit, its boards holding the last of an aging coat of peach paint.

It's still quite early, the ocean is still half-asleep, the palest of blue-greens pushing softly up onto the fine white sand. Maybe Marty won't be here. Maybe she'll be out of town, or already off to work. But of course she'll be here, Jesse knows it. The Fates are usually up for a little drama; they won't be able to resist conspiring to make this moment happen.

She gets out of the car and leans back against a front fender to gather up her expectations. But she finds she has none, actually can't imagine anything will happen today to rub out the past and pencil in something startling and revelatory. This is just something she has to do, an improvised ritual of ablution.

And then the screen door opens and there — after all this time, after all this — there she simply is. Jesse looks up at Marty Finch and feels time warp around the two of them as they stand in its fold. Her first impulse, ridiculous after how much she has gone through to arrive here, is to turn heel and flee, but from there she moves into the dead calm at the eye of her storm. She's ready.

Marty doesn't give off so much as a blink of wondering who Jesse is, or trying to put her into this context, or wondering why she is here — none of the things that happen when you're not expecting someone. Rather it appears she has been expecting Jesse all along, as she leans forward against the railing and moves straight into a smile of pure pleasure, her eyes filled with lies.

Jesse waits to, wants to, hear them.

CPSIA information can be obtained
at www.ICGtesting.com
Printed in the USA
LVHW032108010922
727389LV00003B/252

9 780395 877555